Responsibility

Also by Nigel Cox

Tarzan Presley

Skylark Lounge

Dirty Work

Waiting for Einstein

Responsibility

Nigel Cox

Victoria University Press

VICTORIA UNIVERSITY PRESS
Victoria University of Wellington
PO Box 600 Wellington

First published 2005
Reprinted 2006 (twice)

National Library of New Zealand Cataloguing-in-Publication Data

Cox, Nigel, 1951-
Responsibility / Nigel Cox.
ISBN 0-86473-496-4
I. Title.
NZ823.2—dc 22

Printed by Astra Print, Wellington

for my sister Debbie

Acknowledgements

The author would like to thank Fergus Barrowman, Jo McColl, Bill Manhire, Barbara Polly and Michelle Tayler, all of whom read various drafts of this novel and made helpful suggestions, and the staff of Victoria University Press; Gelia Eisert in Berlin for photography, local research, etc; and Rodney Smith for the cover.

The epigraphs from novels by Charles Willeford are from the *Charles Willeford Omnibus*, reproduced by kind permission of No Exit Press. The poem 'Light' by Geoff Cochrane is from *Nine Poems* (Fernbank Studio, 2002) and is reproduced by kind permission of the author. The Wal-Mart story was found in *Nickel and Dimed: Undercover in Low-wage America*, by Barbara Ehrenreich (Granta Books).

'At the last moment I twisted sideways and brought my right fist up from below my knee. His jaw was wide open and my blow caught him flush below the chin. He fell forward on the floor, like a slugged ox.'

from *Pick-Up*

'She was a large—strapping is a better word—country girl with a ripe figure, cornflower-blue eyes, and a tangle of wheat-coloured hair flowing down her back.'

from *The Burnt Orange Heresy*

'I'm taking eight thousand in cash, and I'm going to lay it fight by fight instead of putting it all down on the outcome. No matter what happens, we'll still have a fifty-fifty chance of coming home with a bundle. Now, just in case we win the tourney, how much will we win?'

from *Cockfighter*

all by Charles Willeford

Chapter One

I'm standing on the little dock above the lake at the bottom of my garden with my wife Bernadette, who is holding our youngest, Sandy, and Fred, five this year, and there are trees hanging down over the water, which is dark, with the reflections of clouds in it, and then out towards the middle a fish jumps. It might rain. I'm holding something like a plastic frying pan, which has a chemical liquid in it and Fred is dipping a circular wand and then flicking it in the air, so as to create streams of bubbles, which tumble away on the gusty it-might-rain wind. In my other hand I also have a wand, but mine has a bigger hole than Fred's, the bubbles it makes are bigger and harder to get. The wind blows into the loop of my wand and drags out a long shape, filmy, wobbling, alive to every current in the air. It takes patience but finally I get a decent bubble made, it's the size of a piglet and is too heavy to fly properly. It wobbles its way down to the surface of the lake and then, to my astonishment, when it hits it bounces, a slow, fat bounce, and gets up again, to fly on just above the water, taking shapes, bouncing, keeping going. It's the most watchable thing as you know that any minute it will be gone. Now a row boat comes into view from the top right and the people in the boat see the bubble and they see us and wave and Bernadette turns Sandy in her arms so that he sees them waving. In the boat there is a little girl, about Fred's age, and the girl and Sandy wave to each other enthusiastically while we adults watch with big smiles on our faces. Then, out near the island, the bubble pops.

*

There was once a girl who used to bring bottles of bubble liquid to the Botanical Gardens, where we would meet and smoke up and intend to have sex except that the smoke always made her so giggly and me so head-fucked that it hardly ever happened. This was back in Wellington; way back. Most commonly we would spend an hour releasing bubbles and into each one I would desperately invest hopes that soon I would start feeling inspired and upright and want to put her hand in my pants, but for that to work there has to be something there for the girl to find and most of the time there was just a limp and feeble thing that lacked sufficient clarity of purpose to show its face. That girl, whose name I can remember, just laughed. There were other guys for her to have botanical sex with, I was good mainly, I think, for a link to an innocence her generation could no longer muster. I was somewhere in my early thirties then and she was maybe nineteen, I had no business, but that year that was my problem, I had no business, no purpose at all, and so I was regressing, smoking again, hanging in a dead-shit job, buying old psychedelic records that I wasn't hip enough to like when they first came out, things like Jerry Garcia's first solo album with *Eep Hour* and *Spidergawd* on it, spooky music that if you'd had enough to smoke made you seriously believe that you would never make fifty; even the next day seemed a stretch. But we all make fifty, nothing can stop us. No matter what you do to your head, Monday morning keeps arriving—this is my accumulated wisdom. *Spidergawd* has a drug policeman-type voice on it that intones *We don't think so*, over and over, which, as the song progresses, becomes *We don't think*—this was, you know, social comment. Which, if I was head-fucked enough, could easily make me start thinking, It's true you know, you really don't think . . .

I'm fifty-one.

When at the lake the rain finally arrived we ran laughing up through the trees and inside, hair wet, shaking ourselves, and there in the house he was, large, wet also, dripping in fact like a hosed dog, grinning, though grin is an inadequate word for the thing that was on his face, which was positive in shape but which leaked messages from less agreeable parts of the spectrum. He was inside our house! He was smoking! He was grinning at us! Bernadette looked from him to me and back again. She is a welcoming person, not like me, and is famously prepared to take on more or less anyone. He let out a heavy fog of smoke—how could anything keep burning in such wet fingers?—and from behind it said, 'Random, man, it's good to see you, man!'

Now the look on Bernadette's face changed; now it was for certain that this was my responsibility. I was aware that, unusually, Fred had got himself behind my legs. Without looking I put a hand down, touched his head to steady him. Or maybe I was steadying myself. 'Stevens,' I said.

This made him sigh. But it was recognition, so he took it as a sign that he should make himself at home and sat down on one end of the green couch so that there would be room, I knew, for him to swing his boots up just as soon as Bernadette wasn't looking. Water ran from him and the coverlet of the couch began to darken. 'Hell finding you, man,' he said.

No one has called me Random for yonks. For years now it's usually been Rummy. But in recent times even that has changed. A woman at work said, in the careful German way, 'I think I will now call you by your first name if that is all right.'

'Yep, that's okay, Martina.'

It was hard to know what to think about the invasion

of Iraq. Naturally I was against it. By nature, I mean. Mine is a nature that didn't want to fight. As a boy I read in the war comics about how the Allied soldiers had to run up the beaches into the face of enemy fire, this was in World War Two, which now sounds like Attack of the Robots Two, and I knew I wouldn't be able to do that. I would disgust my fellows and humiliate my parents by shooting myself in the foot or something—anything to avoid running into those flying bits of death. If those seem like mere words then let me explain that even now thinking about that situation makes me start to sweat. Even now when there's no chance I'll have to go.

As it happens my surname is Rumsfield. Please note the 'i'. Until last year, this name for most people gave images of a paddock, sloping, overgrown, facing the sea, where smugglers hid barrels of rum, of small boats with muffled oars coming in through a sea-mist on nights when cloud obscured the moon. People called me Rummy, they always have. Gin Rummy, which is a nice family game. Rum-soaked, which is somehow a thing to be indulged rather than condemned as alcoholic. Red Rum was of course a big-hearted racehorse.

But Rummy wasn't enough for Stevens. He was always changing the names of things so as to, as he saw it, up the ante. When he introduced me to people as Rumour it was as though they, by accepting the name, accepted his whole manner of procedure. His whole hardboiled, blood-streaked, tumbrel-riding, too-heroic-to-bathe gamut of wank, entire.

Himself he called Shake.

And now he sat on my couch and dripped.

There'd been a pop star in I guess the 1970s whose stage name was Shakin' Stevens and I always presumed this was where he'd got the name, though Shakin' Stevens failed to record anything that even a train-spotter like me can drag to the surface. Of course Stevens himself always denied this—he denied that his name had ever been anything but Shake.

Now he was tapping ash onto the floor. Bernadette said brightly—way too brightly—'I'll make some tea,' and hustled the kids out of the room. As Fred went past I saw that something was holding his eyes so that as he walked his head turned on his neck, keeping it in view—I followed his gaze. It was on Stevens's side. Where his coat had fallen away, where his jacket had been eased back, there, beneath his armpit was a black leather holster with a dark butt of metal protruding from it.

'You packing?' I said.

Well, I couldn't help myself. How many chances in your life do you have really to say that? To say, Reach for the sky! Fill your hands, you sons of bitches.

And Stevens loved it. 'Heat, yeah,' he said, cool as a million. He tapped more ash, took a final puff, then flicked the fag-end over his shoulder, where it landed in the Duplo basket. 'Got to,' he said, and his eyes went back and forth in his head as though checking obscure angles. 'In the present circumstances.'

There was a smell of burning plastic and quickly I went to douse the smoulder that his fag-end had started.

That night in bed as Bernadette and I continued our on-going negotiations about the use of a condom, the sounds of others who had settled this matter came clearly through the wall. 'He's found the late-night porno,' I said. 'I'll get him to turn it down.'

'Make him turn it off!'

'I can't do that.'

'It's disgusting. He is like some revolting thing that crawled in from the swamp. Did you see the way he looked at Sal?'

Yes, I had. Actually, what I had seen was Stevens's tongue, which when Sally entered the room had emerged to make a slow circuit of his purple lips. Sally is my daughter from the bad time between my marriages. She is presently trying in life to be thought of as an experimental film maker who finances her art by turning tricks—thus when Stevens first saw her, the upper part of her body was covered only by a cardigan that had originally belonged to one of her dolls. I could see Stevens finding a place for her in his thinking. 'There was this dangerous little moll, who was like a movie extra trying to work her way into the scene. She had curves that wrenched the steering wheel, eyes like the oasis of sin. I had to fight her off with every inch of my manhood.' Sal is thirteen.

It's true that she went all slinky when she saw Stevens. But, as I tried to tell him, this means nothing, she does it at me if I'm the only one home. But for Stevens this only added to the attraction—'a babe who's gotta have it.' Right there on the premises. I could see him thinking that he might finally have found a place to settle.

Yes, as he sank deeper into the couch I could see Stevens thinking that this might really be the perfect set-up he had been looking for.

I was very afraid.

The next day, when I appeared at work I was unshaven. Well, this sometimes happens. It's nice to be chairing a meeting and to run your hand over your stubble, to think, In an hour I'll be out of here, this isn't my whole life. To think, I haven't been completely sucked in by the system.

But I wasn't kidding myself. The stubble was part of the Stevens effect, where all parts of the landscape are rendered through his proximity down to their flophouse aspect.

Their noir aspect, Stevens would say. He sees the world, he says, through a noir filter, he sees the lurid hinterland, where the base desires have stripped to their edible underwear and are flaunting themselves. But he was himself entirely a base desire, a walking poultice of lust, hunger and greed. Oh, and failure—don't forget failure.

All of this was running through my head, admonitions like a memo to my better self, as I sat in the weekly meeting of the Day One Management Team and pretended that I gave a shit. I'd been in the job too long, we had been in Berlin too long, Bernadette says so every night and she is right, but the money is good and money, well, money is an issue.

Bernadette you see is the last of the big spenders. 'Let's go to Goa,' she says. 'Let's go to Cuba.' And so for two weeks the world is ours, we hire big old cars and go on tour. Bernadette is good at holidays, they're her best thing, and we camp on the beach and lick ice cream off each other's faces. 'Hey, let's go to Greece!' By saying yes to these propositions I convince myself that I am escaping the treadmill, that the unexpected and fabulous can still happen to me. But what I'm really after is a permanent escape. Work was going to be fun, something you chose to do, for kicks—I got hijacked. Yes, I'm getting a good whack. But, the way we go through it, I see that I will still be in harness until Sandy is a graduate.

And Bernadette insisting that we have another.

Stevens on the couch saying to me, 'This one will really be the payday.'

Inka in the Day One meeting saying, 'What do you think, Martin, should we buy these stanchions or hire them?'

And everyone round the table staring at me. 'Buy,' I say

quickly. 'I mean, hire. Yes, I mean hire—anyone object?' They were all really staring. Had I actually been asleep?

Stevens came into my life—you usually say that about a woman, don't you—in 1979 when I had enmired myself in an intense retroactive phase. At the time, as I said, I was smoking a lot and looking for music to go with the smoke. In second-hand record stores I truffled for things like *Electric Music For The Mind And Body* by Country Joe and the Fish—remember, they played at Woodstock?—LPs by Moby Grape and Big Brother and the Holding Company which had been cut during the 1960s. In 1979 punk was turning into New Wave, people like Talking Heads were making terrific music, as I discovered a decade later, but I had my head buried in a poster book with the classic music posters from the San Francisco love-era of the late 1960s. In 1969 my mother, who is a genius, had found this somewhere, Wellington's legendary Unity Books I guess, and had given it to me for my birthday. I was fifteen; it was maybe the last time I was in tune with the zeitgeist. For a whole teenage summer I stayed in my bedroom and stared into the smoke-induced images on those pages. They were collages mostly, in the psychedelic style, with a distinctive type of lettering that writhed or was moulded like putty, making the strange names of the groups they advertised—It's A Beautiful Day—seem like doorways to an alternative reality. (Oh, Alternative Reality: what happened to you?) I made my own posters, in that bedroom, and tried to imagine the music that might go with the images in the book, as in New Zealand it wasn't readily available. This is a classic New Zealand state, I think, to be inspired by something you have read about rather than encountered. The country is so far away, New Zealanders have grown intense imaginations, highly idealistic, based on a utopian, an untested idea of what things—art movements, political radicalisms—might really be like if you were living in them.

Whereas here in Berlin, where everything has already happened . . .

I want to drag this out a bit, I think it's relevant.

My father—my dad, my lovely old dad—once took me from darkest Masterton where we lived over the Rimutaka ranges to Wellington, to a place called the Basin Reserve. Now this was a name I had heard on the radio and to really be going there—I'd just turned ten, as I recall—was exactly the experience I describe above, of finally going to see something that you have heard a great deal about. The Basin Reserve, which is a name I love, is a cricket ground—cricket is a game people cared about, once—and there we were to see an English cricketer named Colin Cowdrey who was at that time utterly famous. My friends and I knew his name from the radio and in our backyard test matches we would take turns at being him. Now I was going to see him, and I was somehow afraid. Of what, I didn't know—the big city of Wellington, maybe? There was that tingling in the under-thought which accompanies any encounter with something long-imagined.

Will it live up?

And at first it seemed as though the tingling was on the money. Colin Cowdrey was just a bloke. I loved the Basin, which turned out to be a smooth oval disk of brilliantly green grass inside a high white fence. It had the drama of an arena, a setting for theatre, and I loved being out with my dad. But Cowdrey was soft-featured, jowly, amiable. Tubby, even. I had expected someone so—I don't know what—big? Dominant? Fabulous, that was not a word we used then, but it was what I expected, and he was just one of the English team, a chap in white flannel—warming up with the other chaps, he could

17

have been my dad. Then, to the huge disappointment of the spectators it was announced over the speakers that he was not actually going to play that day, that he'd hurt himself in the nets or somehow, the details are obscure to me, but what I do remember is the collective groan from that crowd. Maybe I'd never been in a real crowd? The power of everyone releasing an inner response at the same time! We sat squashed together on wooden seats, long and slatted. The day was hot and tiring. But like something brought slowly to the boil the crowd got worked up as, against the odds, New Zealand had England on the run. We were getting their famous batsmen out—little New Zealand, the engine that could!—and the arena air was filled with shouts and sighs. After my early disappointment, I was gradually again filled with a sense of magic. Something was happening! My dad was excited—he turned to me, beaming down, and said, 'Hell, Martin!' Then, late in the day, when the English really had their backs against the wall and New Zealand hopes were at their highest, it was announced that Cowdrey, though injured, would bat. He was by now well down the batting order, at number eight maybe, and when he came out onto the ground his left forearm was in plaster. Maybe it was the left? I don't know. I don't really know if any of this is really true, or, if it is, I am sure all the details are wrong. I could check. But what if it turned out that I have misremembered my life?

Give me wank over weality any day.

And of course Cowdrey batted like a storybook hero. Very quietly, you could hardly see what he was doing. It was all glances and cuts, and this slightly overweight, soft-looking man slowly jogging the length of the pitch. The crowd loved and hated it—that they were seeing this famous artistry, that our hopes of an historic victory were fading. Ah, to be in a crowd and feel its emotion. To be at one with a crowd, that is my greatest longing. As the day drew to a close the shadows of the players lengthened. The green of the grass seemed to acquire a lustre. When at stumps Colin Cowdrey came off, having saved the day, the other players pushed him to the fore and walked behind in a half-circle, clapping. His shadow on the brilliant grass seemed—I can see it now—to be so long: only a giant of a man could cast such a long shadow.

I went home over the Rimutakas with a bigger world inside me.

Anyway: as I said, I was smoking a lot and buying the records that went with those posters that I had never heard—several months of this was enough to turn me into a thing my old friends avoided; who in turn avoided them back, along with my parents, and all authorities and anything that looked like a day of reckoning. This is the state I was in when Stevens came into my life.

When I was recruited. That makes it sound as though I was shoulder-tapped by the CIA. And in fact the process wasn't so different.

I was in an alley alongside the State Opera House, filling my head with smoke before joining a concert by a re-formed band from the sixties called Zoom Miles, when a thing approached me. It was wearing fishermen's boots with trailing laces, a gigantic herringbone coat, a hillbilly's hat pulled down tight and a massive black beard. I was, as I say, in a condition and this thing appearing at my elbow and leaning in really made my heart pound. 'It's cool, I'm not the man,' it muttered. Okay, enough of the it, but he did appear to be more object than human, something clump-like, an overgrown shrub. Later he claimed to have been in disguise, but it was a disguise he often wore twenty-four hours a day.

'I'm private,' he said.

'I'm Martin,' I said and stuck out my hand. Well, I was in a condition.

'I'm a P.I.,' he said patiently, 'a private detective.' I was impressed by this but in my state that was no big feat, I would have been impressed by a tiddlywink. I offered, a bonding gesture, to share my smoke with him but, all seriousness, he brushed it away. 'There's a particular circumstance occurring,' he said, and his voice slipped quite naturally into the tone taken at a briefing by a senior officer. 'In the brown Hunter with the vinyl roof you will see a man in flared jeans—he's mine. What I would like you to do is to take the woman. She has red high heels, you don't have to get too close, you can just follow the sound. You've probably never trailed anyone before—don't sidle. If she looks back, bend down and tie your shoelace.' I was wearing slip-ons but he was in his stride. 'She never goes far, she's not the walking type. Note the address—you've been smoking, so write it down,' he passed me a cheap ballpoint, 'and I'll meet you here after the concert.'

How did he know I was going to the concert? How did he know I'd probably never trailed before? The man impressed me—I probably would have done a good impression of the dog with eyes as big as saucers. Though I could never get my mind around the dog with eyes as big as mill-wheels. If they were that big then how big was his head? If so, how was he able to sit on the chest full of gold pieces, unless it was too big for the soldier to have opened without advanced technological support? Anyone?

I should at this point note that this was the last and only time in my experience of Stevens that he assigned me to the woman. He's a filthy creature, he gets you to be as low as he is, it's his single genius. Whatever, he had filled my circumstantial head with the sound of high heels clicking, red shoes flashing, and flashes of thigh, flashes of stocking-top and a glimpse of a darkening room with pale shadows that came together in well that's quite enough of that but before you knew it I was standing there alone, fingers burning from the roach, the wall behind me thudding to the beat of the warm-up act, teeth fizzing, every shadow seeming to be filled with meaning—and in my other hand I held what turned out to be a ballpoint pen. Where was Stevens? But he had gone as bewilderingly as he had appeared.

Chapter Two

Red Heels and Flared Jeans stayed in the car so long I had to have a second smoke. The wall behind me had gone quiet and I knew that Zoom Miles were setting up. But I had a mission in my head. You know how it is when you're smoking, there is always one thing you mustn't forget. Have fun but don't lose the tickets. Don't forget that the key was to be left under the mat. Remember to remember! Write it on your hand! So I did. In the filthy light of the alley I scrawled 'red hells'—I meant heels, but when I'm smoking literacy can no longer be banked upon—into the flesh of my thumb. A happy little grin tickled my lips: I was so smart. I was going on an adventure. Plus I was going to hear the Zooms. Then I had a rendezvous. After that would come an inspired future of astonishing significance—magic. I was swaying, probably moaning. If the man had turned up—Stevens's lexicon was so noir-dumb—he would have said, Do not pass Go.

Then the car door opened.

I had to restrain an overwhelming impulse to shout to Stevens, 'The car door's opening! Mummy, come and wipe me!' First out was Flared Jeans, he went right, but I didn't care about him, my eyes were mill-wheels for those shoes, which came slowly down from behind the half-open door as though they were the feet of an astronaut, testing the surface of a new planet.

She was sheathed by a long coat, which made her hard to properly assess. But I knew she was gorgeous. It was her disdain. She didn't check the street; she didn't need the street. She didn't need the world. Off she sailed, with me, tongue hanging to the footpath, after her. Staying back a little, as Stevens had instructed, then, anxiety rising, closing in practically to sniffing distance. There was something about her walk, a kind of hesitation in her stride that slowed her and I knew at once that she was some gorgeous creature disfigured by a drunk cunt and a speeding vehicle. She was, I knew, the kind to sneer at her pain, the kind who understood that her accident was a message, a key delivered on a velvet cushion, which had opened the meaning of things to her, while the rest of us ate at the golden arches and voted Labour.

I was not, I knew, fit to pour her a cup of tea.

Manners Street in those years had none of the luxury and majesty you routinely encounter today. Back then it was all chewing-gum birdshits splattering the footpath and parking meters like silver matchsticks, a metal queue waiting for enlightenment. Someone had spewed a map, the street lights fizzed, up ahead the pie cart had attracted a cloud of human flies. Only my mission was pure, and I held to it unswervingly. Her heels carried me—up past Pigeon Park, alongside walls of raw breeze-block. In the blotchy light the textures of everything, concrete, asphalt, were fascinating to me—urban artworks in the eye of an inspired beholder. Everything was fascinating to me. My tongue was out. The heels clicked. I was in a dream. I was saved!

She was stopping.

Inconspicuously, I interviewed a lamppost. Taxis passed, a little movie inside each one. I gazed around as though I was a local, checking the neighbourhood before turning in for the night. She was doing something—my eyeballs came right out of my head and stretched on their strings up the footpath to look into the little handbag where she was fossicking. A key. She began to extend it towards the door which, standing right there in the wall, had previously been hidden to me.

'Stay back!' said a voice of command. This was Stevens, he was off somewhere after Flared Jeans but he was also in my head, directing things. 'Do not approach the suspect!' But I had to go close, I was running a little movie of my own.

I hurried up to her. I didn't want to startle so I made sure my feet slapped. In my head words attempted to arrange themselves into a sentence but pretty women bring out my inner gerbil. I would ask her the time. 'Have you got it?' I blurted. 'Could I just check your wrist?'

She was smiling at me.

She was at least seventy.

But she wasn't slow, she understood at once that I was a harmless fuck-up who wanted no more than the hour. Seventy—more like eighty, her neck in the street lighting was like giblets, like a collapsing tower of wet chicken skin. No, that was my hard. She showed me her wrist. There was something girlish in this, a pretty gesture. It was nine-thirty. As I stared at the dial I knew that it should be telling me something.

She said, 'Can you read it? This is a terrible light, isn't it. I can never find the keyhole, here, let me.' She really was rather sweet. Why wasn't she trembling, this old girl out late on the mean streets. But one glance told her I was pet food.

It's my problem. I'm soap clear through, everyone can see that I will go quietly, will pay and pay and then pay again.

I saw that if I hung any longer she would invite me up for a nice cup of hot Milo. Gently I thanked her and proceeded towards Willis Street. There was something wrong with this, my shoes were smarter than me and wanting to go the other way, but I insisted, which was confusing—my feet tangled and I fell.

I skinned my hands. Actually, I was happy. Happy that she'd been so nice, happy that I was on a mission. Yes, it was good for once to be in something, instead of just dreaming about it.

What was I in?

Stumbling, talking to myself, half-catching myself, stumbling on—in this manner I actually made it to Willis Street and crashed into a bar on the corner. Where, from behind a beer, Stevens eyed me. 'I was expecting you,' he said sourly.

There was something wrong with this also and I imagine that I frowned. I see myself swaying in the entrance light of that bar, no one looking except me—I was always looking at me—and frowning as though I had just received a brick to the head. I looked at my hands—they were skinned and bleeding but that wasn't it. The ballpoint: and it all came back to me. 'Hang on,' I said, and I made a sudden exit. Back down Manners Street. Found her door. Wrote down the number on my hand.

Sauntered back to the bar.

Of course Stevens wasn't there; never had been. Again I stood swaying. Someone approached me, I knew it was the bouncer, they don't like swaying, and I turned beforehand and exited again. Again—this night was turning into the Again Game where you've already done everything, again makes me confused, especially when I'm in a condition.

I wandered the bleak footpaths, seeking inspiration.

Then it came to me: I was meeting Stevens! I turned back to the bar—no. I turned back to the door—no, that wasn't it either. The alley! The concert! The rendezvous—my important rendezvous in the alley after the Zooms! And I ran.

*

Now that time is buried deep, heaped over with garlic, a stake through its heart. I am a reformed person, a changed man, and what's more I have managed to swing this without becoming a bible basher. Proud? I guess so.

Sometimes, at the Memorial, when I am being talked to by, say, the visiting head of another memorial site in, oh, Stockholm, I notice that he's taking notes. We're at a table in the courtyard, the hoff the Germans call it, with the Berlin sun streaming down, the trees a blaze of green, summer girls are everywhere and so are my eyes, measuring midriffs— and I see that this guy is impressed by me. This is always a terrific shock. He's much better dressed, in standard-issue culturewear, dead-black with the interesting tie, terrific shoes, terrific haircut, the manager with aesthetics, and he has, from his inside pocket, produced one of those small black notebooks with an elastic to keep the pages neat and now in this notebook he's inscribing something. Probably it's just, 'How did this clod get this job?' but even that would be impressive because, what do they speak in Stockholm, Swedish I guess, and so he's writing in Swedish while he's talking to me in English, he ordered for us in German, he's a Doktor or whatever they call that in Sweden, he's been an archaeologist and has done, I dunno, a yard's worth of distinguished things—and he's taking me seriously. It's astonishing. So I pull myself together, try to guess what might have come out of my mouth in the last few minutes, try to actually say something. And to my amazement this only causes increased note-taking. Okay, I'm being hard on myself, but there's more than a grain of truth here: I can't believe that I, once a pale pool of wank, might somehow have ended up in this position. You think I'm being modest? Okay, check this out: Swedes are one thing, a country like that with nothing to do except sex, that's one thing, but I have had my words go into the notebooks of Australians! That is gospel. Culture-industry people from Perth, Sydney and the Black Stump have paid their respects to me—a New Zealander! Australians don't *do* respect.

I could go on a bit here about how finally I made the A-team but is it really to your credit that for once in your life you lucked out?

Anyway, I think the subject of interest right now is Stevens. That's what's got me going. It's interesting, he's a catalyst. I would never have thought that.

The next night, after the Duplo fire, I caught a certain look in Bernadette's eye and said, 'Stevens and I will go out for pizza.' This was acceptable to the look. Bernadette hardly knows a soul in Berlin, she needs me to unload on over dinner, but not with Stevens. So we went. The kids kicked up; they like pizza too, when I left they were screaming. I knew that later, when I got into bed, Bernadette would hit me, bang, her little fist hard in the dark, and then turn her back. After a while she would say, coldly, You stink of cigarettes. And, Get him out of my house.

But she believes in hospitality and, anyway, she had seen the panic in my eyes.

So, out of the house: the gate clangs behind us, we're off—I indicate that we'll be going right. But Stevens won't and I have to stop. He's by the gate, looking baleful. What does that mean, really, full of bale? Must look it up. Maybe I've got the wrong word, I mean that he's bad-eyeing the street. I guess the feeling is mutual—that particular street doesn't I imagine think too much of him. Zehlendorf is where Berlin's doctors come to die, where the city parks its black Mercedes and Opels. It's so slumberland hereabouts that every time one of our kids utters a peep they send round a delegation. You think I'm kidding but when baby Sandy pulled the head off a tulip in someone's garden Bernadette got a home visit from an ashen-faced woman saying, 'I am also a foreigner and I know how these little things can grow into something very large in this country so I thought I should speak to you now before the situation becomes quite serious: your child must not do that.' Oh dear.

Anyway, Stevens is hanging onto the gate so I go back—going close means going within pong-distance of him, which is not a good idea—and ask, 'What's the story?'

His eyes have a There's-something-I-cannot-look-at cast, his head is inclined as though he's being pulled by the hair. 'Other way,' he mutters, and heads off to the left. 'Make like you know me,' he mutters. What he means is that I'm hanging back, reluctant—well, I like pizza and every step is taking me further from it; also, I am not feeling chummy—but I do as I'm told, I go alongside him and we saunter, close enough to hold hands. It's a nice night for a walk, not quite dark yet, and springtime in Berlin while not exactly springtime in Paris is nevertheless a sweet thing. The grey city, burdened by its past, suddenly lights up. People come out and tilt their faces upwards. It's the trees, which, bursting into leaf, make your heart expand. You let out that breath you didn't know you were holding in. Birds seem to be messengers, flying lines, full of purpose, instead of fellow combatants in a grim struggle. There are squirrels, like animated punctuation. Walking now with Stevens I would be full of the joys. But he is grim-faced and will only speak in a mutter.

'Never indicate which direction you're going,' he instructs in an undertone. 'It's like you've forgotten everything, Rumour. Walk around the block, remember, see if anything follows.'

Well, as I said, it's a nice night out. We amble along Argentinische Allee, turn left at the little path with the wooden seats where the kids from the big houses sneak out to for a fag. Amble towards the bridge, which can be seen up ahead, between the parallel lines of trees and bushes which make a sort of leafy tunnel. Stevens bends to tie a shoelace, but it wasn't loose, anyone can see he's checking rearward. He's such a ham. Openly, I turn around and take a look. Nothing. Well, why would there be.

Suddenly from the dark of the bushes on our right a dog bursts and confronts us, barking up, ears back, feet planted—I can see right down its pink throat. What kind of dog? Haven't got a clue, dogs are just shitting machines as far as I'm concerned—something big and floppy. Anyway, this dog prompts Stevens to whip out his gun. Using both hands he takes aim at its tonsils. His arms are stiff, with his long coat thrown back he looks like Clint E in *The Good, The Bad and The Ugly*. But the dog prefers Fassbinder—it trots up and sniffs the barrel. Stevens's eyes are narrowed, his lip is on the curl, I can see he's thinking of killing this dog for disrespect and I give him a get-moving nudge—so the gun goes off.

God, it's loud. The nudge means that the bullet misses the dog, ricochets off the path and whizzes up into the evening sky.

Stevens makes us walk. I can't hear our footsteps, I can't hear anything, I'm deafened by the bang, but I just know that every window for miles around is opening. We stumble along to the bridge, stop, and gaze down at the water. I am so filled with dread that I am clear-headed. Stevens is going to leave town, Bernadette is right about everything—we can even have another baby. I am not getting entangled with him. If I could have had a shave, put on a tie, I would have done it, right there on the bridge.

But Stevens doesn't give a damn. He is now deeply in

character and bullshit guides his every move. The bridge has metal railings, he puts his hand through them, he's holding a stick and he drops it, as though he's playing Poohsticks. Goes to look; comes back and drops another. In dropping a third stick he also deals with the gun—he has found a little ledge under the bridge, the flat of an I-beam, and here he places the thing, tucked away out of sight. Then he drops a final stick and makes a big finish of crossing the bridge for the last time. Well, it's an old trick but it just might work.

When I look back the dog is standing foursquare in the middle of the path, head tilted, looking pointedly at us.

We stumble on. The police arrive—terrific. They have a van and we get into it and are interviewed. My heart is so loud that the metal walls of the van are banging.

It's weird this, that the German police make you get into the back of a van, there's a table, it's somehow cosy. They sit across from you and it seems like someone is about to produce a tumbler of wine. But this is not a chummy occasion.

However, Stevens has his passport and I have, in my wallet, my registration papers, which prove that my home is just up the road and this makes us seem like locals, despite my German, which stumbles and blurts. Plus I have the wit to also produce my ID from the Memorial and this I see is an object which commands respect. They are serious about history in this country—well, you would be, wouldn't you. Nevertheless they are intent on having us empty our pockets and I can see that at any moment they'll find the shoulder-holster—why get rid of the gun but not the holster?—and my heart threatens to tear my house down. But Stevens asks if he can have a cigarette. And this is somehow a turning point— they don't give out cigarettes to the public, we're wasting their time, they don't want anything to do with us; go, go, we're busy. So we go, asap. As we are doing so suddenly there's a

30

question. We both become entirely unable to understand a word that is spoken to us. So one of the policemen, the fat one, points to his gun, makes a bang sound, then puts his hand to his ear and makes the looking-for face. The other cop is watching us—why can't he see that Stevens's left elbow is tucked in like it's stuck to his side? But the fat cop's dumb show is funny and we laugh, which is not okay, and angrily they see us off. Phew.

But definitely I am about to become a father again.

The pizza tasted like cardboard. This had nothing to do with the cooking, which as usual was superb, but was entirely the product of the Sahara inside my mouth. Stevens was all cool (if you overlooked the melted cheese in his beard), smoking, eating and drinking up large. He'd finally fired his gun! His next project was its retrieval. 'Your property backs onto a lake,' he said, getting the words out as he shunted the pizza in, 'and it's the same lake as under the bridge, right—we'll just paddle along, climb up and get it.' He didn't even ask if we had a boat. Strangely enough, we did, an inflatable that I had bought cheap so Fred and I could go fishing. But my head was shaking so hard that even Stevens got the message.

The restaurant had a fence of iron stakes, tipped with sharply pointed little tongues, and a fringe of trees, we were out in the night, in a private courtyard where, beneath a tilting moon, delicious food could elegantly be consumed. I loved coming to this place. But Stevens was putting me off in a big way. He can really louse up a neighbourhood.

While we were waiting for his second pizza to arrive I finally got my question out: 'So how come you're here?'

*

Once Fred and I were out in the rubber boat, floating, pretending to fish, just drifting on the mirror of the lake, and we made it down to that bridge. As we went under he glanced up and then he whispered, 'Look, Dadda.' There was a swallow's nest up under there and, while we watched, the birds came and went. It took some fancy flying to come in over the water, make an unexpected loop because we were there, another loop deciding we were okay, a third loop to go to the nest and suddenly, from fast-flying speed, to stand, quivering, still, on skinny legs, on the lip of the nest. I dipped my paddles quietly and for maybe quarter of an hour we watched.

It's funny with Fred, he has my eyes and that is the single most strange thing I have ever seen in my life. It's not a reflection. It's not a photograph. To have your own eyes looking right back at you out of someone else's head, a head with all of Bernadette's stuff in it too, mixed with mine, to know that that head is different than yours, but then to see those eyes. And to see how they are young. What they look like provokes a shiver of memory, as they are my own eyes as I remember them, I guess from mirrors, forty-six years ago. When I look into them I remember living in rural Rataono: the gravel road that divided the landscape, sheep like white bushes against the green, in the distance a dog barking; then silence. The sound of the creek. A skylark calling down. Indifferent cow. Five-year-old me listening amid the hills of backblocks New Zealand and asking my lonely mother, 'Who can I play with?'

Fred's hair is a colour that can never be painted. It's full of shadows and light, it's thick like a field of hay, it's got depth and substance. I love putting my fingers in it; of course, it's always dirty, unwashed, and also unbrushed—Bernadette never brushes it and brushing is not my department. Noticing is my department.

I'm a terrible father. I guess you've picked that up. Fred wants to go fishing but I'm never available. He wants to do carpentry with me but I never want to. What I want, apparently, is for him to sit beside me on the couch and listen while I give expert commentary on the TV sport. Is that really what I want? I've seen other sons do it, it always looks terrible, but when I'm on the couch and he hoves into view I pat the space beside me. He often comes. He looks and then asks, 'Who do you want to win, Dadda?' But he gets bored and goes off, to do fishing-substitutes, instead-of-carpentry.

But I love him, utterly. Can I claim that? When I pray, and I do, always asking for something and of course not *to* anyone—when I pray I find that without intending it I always start by saying, Keep my children safe; make them happy. It's no contest, the kids are what stand at the middle of your heart, they are there where you used to be—and you abuse them as you have always abused yourself.

Well, it's only fair, I guess.

Yeah, it's a hard world and they better get used to it.

But then I am afraid for them. These days, when I cry in movies, suddenly it's for fear of what might happen to the kids, of what their eyes might be forced to see—the breaking news of a world broken open. Having them has made me squeamish about blood scenes and trauma. Sometimes I wonder if this is just a worry about what people might say— *He let his son drown.* Then into my mind comes an image of him lying lifeless, on a riverbank, me over him, and I get a wrench in my guts that is like a jolt from a socket.

And now Stevens is here, in my life, and at every moment I am feeling more watchful.

*

He eats pizza as though it's unicorn ham, as though it's dragon's eggs, a slice of the sun. Such a gourmand. He's oblivious to the ash he has flicked everywhere, to him the whole world probably tastes like ash. His eyes are way too small, set back inside rings in his head, dead tadpoles lying at the bottom of a jar of weed and slime.

His enthusiasm is vile.

And yet something in him connects with something in me. I am terrified to admit this, or to scrutinise it. Half-grimly, half-eager, I order another beer.

Finally I get my question out. 'So how come you're here?'

He chews this over—I'll spare you the details. His eyes slide left then right, checking that CNN and co have their microphones ready for his statement. 'Okay, Rumour,' he says, 'this is the thing.'

And my worst fears are confirmed. There is a thing, and, to my horror, I am interested in it.

'I had this case, see,' he said, 'with all kinds of aspects, very complex, involving a new tax dodge and a guy who seemed to have lost a leg. This guy, let's call him Roger, had found a house where you couldn't spy on him, way up, not unless you had a chopper. And even if you flew right up outside his window he'd hear you coming,'—his eyes narrowed, I could see Stevens visualising all this crap—'and he'd go and strap his leg up and then stand there like he was Queen's evidence. Very subtle guy—okay, so there's Roger, who owed me.' He placed the salt shaker directly in front of him on the table. 'Also there was this tempting woman, let's call her Diana, she was kind of the huntswoman type, had a big leather coat that she'd whip open when she thought you were losing interest, all kinds of trouble back in there,' he gave a filthy laugh, and his black tongue appeared and went lap-lap. Next to the salt he now placed the pepper. 'So, Diana owed Roger and couldn't settle, not in the cash sense anyway, but she called Preed—Rumour, you breathe a cunting word of this to anyone I'll totally kill you!' Suddenly he was glaring at me across the table. His face turtled forward on his neck and he went into my eyes. Then, slowly, he leaned back and flexed his shoulders. His left elbow lifted and where his coat came away from his body I could see the holster. His eyes went down to it and then back to mine, connecting the two.

Of course the holster was empty and so were his eyes.

But he didn't know that and he leaned in slowly, so that his face came towards me, swelling, as though a camera was moving in. Eyes full of nothing, eyes full of bullshit and chickenshit and horseshit, it was wall-to-wall dung in there, his beard in the pizza, and a halo of little flies, which seemed to have arrived like a special effect, dancing round him in the moonlight. He stared at me and through the curtain of shit, it really was raining down in there, through the shit I saw that he was serious about this and then I really was afraid.

I laughed nervously—all the heavy eyeball stuff was getting to me—and Stevens took this for a sign and whipped his head from side to side as if to spy a creeping attacker. When there was no one he leaned back and scornfully regarded me.

After a long moment he said, a king speaking down from his throne, 'Are you sure that you really want in on this?'

And I did. That was the frightening thing. I did.

Chapter Three

There is a poet in Wellington—I say this to myself as though it's a line: There is a rose in Spanish Harlem. There is a poet in Wellington, and his poems stalk the streets. Except that after Spanish Harlem it should be, There is a poet in Wellington harbour, that would scan better, though that makes it sound as though he's drowning and, in the case of this guy, drowning has a troubling hint of too much liquid. But he can really write a poem. I know what you're thinking, I know what you're thinking, you're thinking that he writes lyrical stuff about clouds and how their shadows passing are like our days which travel forever up the hillsides of our youth . . . Okay, when *this* guy writes about clouds he writes *Tin Nimbus*. That's the name of one of his books and I like to think about this name and have it around the place, like interesting furniture in the living room of my head, an objet d'art. Here's one of his poems:

LIGHT

It dwells in the desert
where it is served
by faceless gods of clay

It lives on her lip

You didn't think I was a poetry guy, did you. And the truth is, I'm not. But with this one poet—it's good to say that word and mean it—I make a point of finding out if he has published a new book and getting hold of a copy. His name is Geoff Cochrane.

Actually *Tin Nimbus* isn't poetry, it's a novel, about drying out. Geoff Cochrane was a drinker, in Wellington, once, back in the days when I was having my fit of regression. One of my fits. *Set The Controls For The Heart Of The Sun*, that's what I was listening to, along with *Heart Beat, Pig Meat* and *Several Species Of Small Furry Animals Gathered Together In A Cave And Grooving With A Pict*, etc. That particular music was by that time at least fifteen years out of date but, the state I was in, this was less than a detail. Then one morning to my alarm I found myself in what is called an 'early opener,' which is a pub that opens at 8am, for those on shift work, or those whose thirst is an early morning thing, or for those who are just thirsty all the time. I have never really been a drinker. A woman of my acquaintance who at 22 was an alcoholic once said to me as we strolled past a bottle store, 'You don't know what it's like, to stand there and look at the bottles and feel your mouth go dry.' And she was right, I don't.

The poet did. He was in the early opener, along with Stevens, whom I was meeting, and he was clearly in his element. I don't mean he was declaiming. It wasn't a declaiming sort of pub. He gazed around with an eye that was both sere and serene, bringing desiccation to all that it fell upon, then watered his throat. It was Stevens who was mouthing off.

I have looked among his poetry for a reference to myself; in vain. You might think this strange, since I met him only the once. But bear with me. The poet wore a corduroy jacket that was aromatic in a way that suggested a life pursued in livid undergrowth. He eyed you as though figuring how many rounds you might be good for—I'm sure this is unworthy. His face was grey, purple, not encouraging, but there was also the beginnings of a lined severity in it which, in the years which followed the taming of his thirst, made him a writer I wanted to read.

Around him in the bar examples of the human species were assembled as though in a statue garden established to discourage human reproduction. Each table was surrounded by silent men twisting their bodies so that they were all open throats pointing to the sky. I was frankly afraid and clutched my glass of beer as if I intended to take it home with me. Stevens also felt it was my function to provide any cash that was required. I was only too happy, as long as I didn't have to drink, or look, or breathe.

Is this how I was going to end up?

When I returned with a third round of fresh jugs he finally said to me, 'So what's your report?'

I had spent the night preceding on a stake-out, that's what he'd called it, in my car, outside a house in a quiet street in the suburb of Lyall Bay: sand-in-the-gutters Wade Street. My instructions, passed to me with maximum security by Stevens the night before as we'd exited from a surf movie, were written on a deposit slip from a bank. I'd been in the bank with him when he wrote them, he could have just told me. 'Wade Street, number 23, white house, a tall guy driving a white Citroën Light 15, wears a white suit, note what time he arrives, anyone who comes, anything that happens. Follow him when he leaves. DON'T LET HIM SEE YOU. Meet at the Champion, Waring Taylor Street, 8.10am to report.'

A stake-out is fun. You push the driver's seat as far back as it will go, slide down it so that no one will see you, and, eyes level with the dash, notice everything in an inconspicuous fashion. After an hour of the National Programme you change stations, then light up a smoke to enhance your observational powers. Then you get hungry. Keeping the target house squarely in the middle of your rear-vision mirror you roll down the street and buy as many Energy Bars as the late-night dairy on the corner will allow. Back on station you drop the wrappers out the window then realise that so many wrappers is a clue that you've been there a long time—you're hugely alert to clues. So you get out, collect them and bring them back into the car. But what if someone glances in, they'll see them, so you get over into the back seat—keeping one eye on the target house, of course—and stuff them down into that crack in the seats where you search for lost coins before you sell the car. Then you need to pee. To the strains of *Sad Eyed Lady Of The Lowlands* (choosing the tapes for a stake-out can take longer than the stake-out itself) you heroically think that you will hold on until this song ends—man, Bob Dylan can write long songs. All nonchalance, you get out to unobtrusively pee against a lamppost. While you are in the middle of your relief you realise that the car door is open and that clouds of smoke are billowing from it—another clue. It's hell walking while you are peeing but you manage it, hardly getting any on your trousers, and shut the door, a bit loud but you only had one hand. Then you see that this has trapped the smoke inside the car and that from the outside it looks as though the fire brigade will be necessary. Innocently, you fan the doors.

By now everyone in the street knows you are there and people are coming out in their night attire to study you, the most interesting thing that has happened round here for years. Shouldn't children all be in bed? But don't get me started on children.

As it turned out number 23 wasn't white.

Over time I came to suspect that Stevens sent me on these missions just to keep me in the game. On that occasion no Citroën ever appeared and a white suit in Lyall Bay would stop the traffic for a decade. But I was never sure. I always stayed until the appointed hour, I always made notes, as instructed, in my notebook: '3am—nothing. Oh, a white cat.'

In the bar of the Champion I delivered my report verbally: 'Suspect never sighted,' but Stevens wasn't satisfied and demanded to see my notebook. He made a big play of scrutinising each line. *2am—nothing*. He read it out. He massaged his chin. Finally he handed it back and said, 'Okay, I have to think.'

It was then that the poet entered the play. 'Could I see the page?'

He read it aloud. Now, utterly deadpan, it sounded like something.

> Eleven pee em—arrived at station
> Midnight—nothing
> One ay em—nothing
> Two ay em—nothing
> Three ay em—nothing. Oh
> A white cat.
> Four ay em—nothing
> Five ay em—nothing
> Six ay em—nothing
> And now
> I am going home.

He asked if he could have the page and gravely tore it out. I buy all his books but he has never published it.

When after the pizza I got home I found Bernadette and Sandy together in our bed. The blind was up—these houses have roll-down blinds, with a loop of strap inside and the blind outside, so that you can shut the place up as though it's a shop, against riots or a sudden attack of the Swamp Creatures—and in the light coming in from the street I could see the story of the night in the way their bodies were lying. His feet were angled towards her hip, his body lay away at a vector. This was because she was trying to escape him; on the pillow, her head was turned away. But he had his hand out. Her teeshirt was up, one pale breast was exposed and, possessively, he had his hand on it. The bedclothes were like the heaped evidence of a battle—in the morning she would groan and say, 'Terrible night.'

Sandy. Fred. Bernadette. Sally. My family—an utter amazement to me.

And now Stevens was among us. How was I going to tell her?

Normally if I come in late like this I sleep on the couch. Inevitably she accuses me of wanting to dodge the battle, but this is unfair. So much of a marriage is unfair—let God be my witness. My good intentions set against our marriage which is, at worst, a path to Hell. No, a path *in* Hell. Here we go now: a path through Hell, with children lying in troubled sleep on either hand, bedclothes sliding, and the rooms all soft shadows, because everyone is afraid of the dark—doors as you go down the path through Hell that swing open to reveal mountains of damp washing, basins smeared with hardened toothpaste, mirrors also, and nests of old floss, an exhaustion of nappies. The kitchen with every surface cluttered, and stacked, and smeared, every cupboard door hanging open, and in the cupboards: Hell! Can a man find his nailclippers in this fucking jumble sale? Let alone his passport. The place routinely looks as though someone told forty thieves that a valuable diamond is hidden here and they have ten minutes. Okay, let me at this point rip off a few licks against Bernadette. I know you've been thinking I'm a kind of nice guy, immature, dopey, but loves his kids, a trier, and with a taste for the lyrical—did you notice that? But let me tell you. I have been keeping something back: the Swamp Creature. But why should I? The truth is the truth, and here is a woman who when faced with a mouldering pile of half-dry laundry will say, straight-faced, 'But I was never trained in how to hang out washing.' Who does on-line crosswords amid the attack of the broken toys, the lament of the dirty dishes. Meanwhile, which of us does the ironing around here? Muggins! Who is the only person ever to lug out the rubbish? To wipe up those ominous food spills which every day are a deeper colour? Who pays the bills? If the fucking bills can only be found. Who brings home the wherewithal? Yes, who makes our trains run on time? I ask you. And who, on the other hand, who for christ sakes is responsible when you open the fridge and there's seven, count 'em, seven pottles of cottage cheese and not so much as a saucer of milk for coffee? Ah, don't get me started.

My lovely Bernadette, that's who. How oh how am I going to tell her?

But it's true, about how we live. You think I am an anal jerk who wants everything *House & Garden* but it ain't so. I like a happy mess. That is all that matters: happiness. I really believe that, I really live that. And I think we are happy, in our terrible muddle. We live as though Bernadette and I are retarded, I often think this, as though we both were raised in some terrible trailer park and don't know any better. 'If the Welfare see this,' is a joke between us, but beneath the joke there is actual fear.

And beneath the fear: happiness. Bernadette says it's all hopeless and makes me feel that mine is the task of keeping us going. But it's a task I believe in. If this ends then we will know, finally, what happiness was.

So how oh how am I going to tell her?

I will tell her it's for the best. Because it is. That's what I have decided and sometimes it has to happen—one partner has to make a decision on behalf of the marriage, know its best interests—we know a guy who bought a house without consulting his wife and that turned out well. Yes, I will remind her of that, and also I will mention the money. If we have money, I will say, then all kind of options come onto the table . . .

Now I think that I will hold *back* the mention of the money. That will be the best thing. Let her shout at me for a bit and *then* mention the money. Only through money might she get another baby. Okay.

But I can't sleep on the couch, because that's where Stevens is sleeping, so I have to join the battle in the double bed. Before I do I take hold of the strap by the window and, as quietly as possible, start to ease the blind down. It creaks. Slowly the street-lamp brightness is closed away from the room. As the last inches of light are being blinded away, Bernadette's mouth opens and, eyes shut, she speaks. The skin of her eyelids looks so pale. She says, 'I can smell you from here.'

I didn't say we had a keller, did I.

I associate this word with the Beatles. Their Cavern in Liverpool was a cellar—wasn't there a song that talked about 'A cellar full of noise'? Yes—by swingin' Petula Clark. And then that cellar is all mixed up with the German keller, which is exactly right for the Beatles, because they got their start in Hamburg, three hours north of here. I should make

43

a sentimental journey. In fact every German house has a keller and this time ours was two actual rooms, each one the size of a good bedroom. From our previous apartment we had a huge piece of grape-coloured carpet which had to go somewhere, and a spare couch. I cleaned out the cobwebs, stacked all our junk in room number one, and, in room two I would . . . get away from the kids! It's a notion I've read about, the shed at the bottom of the garden, where Dad has his radio, and bottle of something and a few old *Playboys*, which he hardly ever flicks through with the door closed. 'Go and tell Dad it's time for dinner.' In your dreams, Dad.

For a start, the kids liked it down there too, especially if I was there.

I installed a standard lamp with a shade like a dancer's tutu, and a wine rack, tried to make it homey. And there it was, another world, under our feet, just waiting for the perfect CD to be played in it.

Oh, I'm avoiding. And there's nothing to avoid, you've long guessed. Everyone knows, it's so bloody obvious.

Everyone except Bernadette.

After a bit of a think I decided to let her find out for herself. 'Oh, that,' I'd say, 'sorry, I thought you knew. I thought you must have observed—you're always so good at noticing things, darling.' Yeah, and then I'd dodge the slap. Not that she really slaps me but, you know, the flying dogbox.

For a while Sal thought she might set up shop in the keller. I haven't said much about Sal, either, have I. It's tricky. She's just thirteen and, as I said, in her vamp phase. Which figures. She was a teenager when she was eight—screamed at us, bought junk perfume, played boy-band CDs at max, began to punk up her Barbies. Now the Barbies are wrapped in tissue paper, waiting for when they're valuable. Now she thinks she's Louise Brooks.

Sal is the walking, talking reminder of a year I had with a woman called Briar Lane, who is out there somewhere in the silky night, the velvet dawn. Briar was the all-sex girl that every man just has to have somewhere on his CV. Never mind that she was a wrecker and everyone could see it. Never mind that she was a huge binge drinker with no fear of tomorrow: if you could only get another turn in the skin with her, then something utter would be transferred to you. Something ur. Something cowboy. If you could only log up enough skin time with Briar your walk would be improved forever—you could talk to gypsies and merchant bankers both, you could be caught in the rain and it would be noble, poetic, instead of just wet. Sex with Briar made you want more sex with Briar. Oh, those famous fucks! Men don't talk to one another about sex, nor do they talk to their women about it. No, the idea is that your back catalogue is something you wear, like a victory shirt. No, even that's wrong. No, your sexual history is something that's *in* you, an accumulated thing, like experience. That's it, exactly that: experience. After sexing with Briar you would drive home—wallet empty, over the limit and starting to figure what excuses you might make—and, deep inside, your inner man would be saying, Good boy! You got me some of the real stuff that time!

Hence Sally, who lived with Briar for eight years and then came to me. Need I say fucked up? At that time Bernadette was pregnant with Fred and it was obvious that instead of a couple we were going to be a family, and what's one more in a family?

Finally it was Sal who did the keller job for me.

We were sitting up, this was three nights after the pizza, in the big room (who has a lounge these days? Drawing room? Sitting room? You know what I mean—the one with the TV) and the lights in the garden had just come on. This is kind of a sylvan setting, you hardly ever use that word, but we do live among trees, with long apartment blocks, like strips of Lego, and there's lights which come on automatically as dusk shifts into dark. The lights are low, just above your head, saucer-shaped and casting a soft white glow that makes old smokers like me think of the arrival of alien spacecraft. Now out among the trees something black and solid moved and Bernadette, looking up from her book, said, 'What was that?'

'I didn't see anything.' Which I didn't.

I made like I was going to draw my shoulders up and go out and face the night but Sal said, 'It was your friend, whatsisname—Shake.'

Bernadette was nonplussed for a moment, but only a moment. 'You mean . . . that pig?'

Bernadette can do a very good pained expression when she wants to, and what is remarkable about it is that it transfers its pain to you. I began to experience difficulty with my breathing.

'I like him,' said Sal. And she arched her spine so that the front of her teeshirt was stretched. Then she returned to painting her nails.

'What's he doing back here?' said Bernadette, low, concerned.

'I'll go and see.'

'He's just getting in the window,' said Sal. She said this so simply, sweetly even. When there is tension between Bernadette and me, Sal is like a kind of Greek chorus, she underscores statements or else offers a new fact, to keep things moving. Her head goes back and forth as though she's at Wimbledon, with the same set of expressions—shock, delight, awe—on her face. Now she giggled. 'Must be a struggle for him.'

A penny had slipped off the edge of a cloud and now,

having swiftly fallen twenty thousand feet, was arriving in Bernadette's head. She looked at me, eyes full of comprehension. Then she looked down, in horror, as though beneath her feet flood waters were rising. 'What?' she said. She took in Sal's face, then mine. Her eyes began to narrow.

Sal said, 'Actually, he's made it all nice, I said I'd visit him. Bern, is there any chocolate?'

Bernadette hates her name, she says it gives away too much about her, she says that people think of Bernadette Devlin but I always say, Only people of a certain age, dear, and if they're of that age, my darling, why don't they think of *Bernadette* by the Four Tops—tell the world! That is a shout of passion, I say, and for me it's the truer reference, I love her name, the burn of it, and the debt, its soul-fire qualities—its uprightness and also its contours, it's like a landscape (the Bernadette hinterland, I can see that), but it is true that it's a hard name to shorten gracefully. She has all her life fought 'Bernie', more or less successfully (there is one cousin who knows how Bernie pains her), and Bern has a hint of that, which Sal, ramping up the volume to perfection, has now triggered. 'None? Okay, I'll take him a beer, his fridge hasn't arrived yet.'

She collects two bottles, flounces out, off the front of the patio, and disappears to the lower right. Leaving me there, stranded. Bernadette says, 'Sal will be climbing down.'

There is such bitter fury in this that I take a moment to see what she means. 'Oh, right,' I say. Sal's skirt is what we used to call decent by no more than an inch, and Stevens will be looking up. 'I better go,' I say and head towards the door.

'And don't come back.'

47

Chapter Four

I would like at this point to go on for a bit about the Beatles and maybe also the Electric Prunes, whose *I Had Too Much To Dream (Last Night)* was very formative for me, but the rest of that evening was something I should force myself to remember.

It had started okay. First Bernadette and me in the TV room reading with Sal there humming away—very pleasant. Then the interlude in the keller. This had a certain Stevens quality. For example, he had cleared a space in front of the red leather couch and there Sal sat, me also, on the floor, while he was enthroned, flicking ash on us like benedictions, allowing us to be thrilled by glimpses of his navel, a black plughole between the about-to-pop buttons of his shirt. Sal's navel too was a presence, of an entirely different sort. A blind eye, a knot in polished wood, a spiral staircase going down to a palace of pleasure, Sal's navel and the honeyed tummy which surrounded it gave off a delicate glow of promise which ennobled the air, at the same time as adding just that spritzig touch of jailbait.

This is the Stevens effect, which can have a father thinking such things about his daughter.

We drank the beer, Sal sipping from my bottle for form's sake, me drinking fast so that she wouldn't get too much, while we were treated to excerpts from a work-in-progress called My Disconnected Ramblings About Nothing In Particular—I'll spare you. Then I pushed her up the ladder.

Ladder? Where did that come from? But it didn't pay to ask.

Out the window: my, but the night air can be bracing.

I saw Sal into her bunk, got my teeth clean, all the while working on a strategy for the Bernadette situation. If I slept on the couch, that would mean I didn't have to face her. But that would only make the postponed showdown even worse. If I went in now and got in with her, then she couldn't raise her voice for fear of waking Sandy.

But she emerged from the bedroom and, in a long pale nightdress, cornered me in the kitchen.

It's the smallest room in the house, with a mock-marble bench on three sides that leaves the bit where you can actually stand as a kind of hole in the middle. A pit. That bench is like the ropes of a boxing ring, you can lean back but you can't get away. Here, by the low light from the range hood, we circled.

I can't tell you what was worse, when she looked at me or when she turned her back. I think the part played by the back in marriage is underestimated. In bed, it can be the Great Wall of China. At the beach, bent like a hoop over a paperback, it can be where you see that the skin of your beloved is the great canvas that life paints upon—ahem, but you know what I mean. The moles and freckles, so tenderness-inducing. Back-rubs, lower back pains, lying back-to-back in the garden while the kids are taking pickaxes to each other, the back makes up for its lack of eyes by being, like a cliff, a face where you can look and read deep. It wasn't, as she bent now over her Milo, stirring slowly, that Bernadette's back was cold to me. Oh, there was chill about her shoulders, but it was down the line of her spine that I saw a concern, a genuine anxiety. 'Okay, I'll keep an eye on her,' I said.

'Who?'

Our voices were low, it's a habit you get into once you have kids, which made the strain worse. 'Sally,' I said. 'I know you're worried about her.'

She turned and got me in her sights. 'Sally at least knows when to come in out of the rain. It's you I'm worried about.'

I had the Kraut version of Jif and was scrubbing ardently at the bench top. Well, it gives you something to do with your hands. 'Darling, he's a friend,' I said. 'A bit of a pig, but a friend—I had to. Anyway, there might be something in it for us.'

'Herpes?'

'Darling, listen.' I pulled myself together a bit, there's always something manly to avail yourself of when discussing finances. 'We can't afford to go home—we've been over this—until we can carry away at least a hundred thousand.'

Her eyes pinned me. 'How much did you give him?'

'Darling, come on, I'm not stupid.'

'Is that in the small print?'

I laughed but she wouldn't catch it. Always at the worst moments she will suddenly laugh, it's her best quality, it takes me by surprise, that she can get to a laugh when the floor is falling from under. But she wouldn't. So I said, into her stone face, 'We've got seventy thousand to go and if this works out we'll get it in one hit.'

'Why don't you say, *When* this works out?' This was said bitterly but in fact I could see I had her attention.

'Look,' I said, breathing easier, 'there's a scam. A famous con, you might even have heard of it, called the Nigeria Scam.' Now the explaining voice kicked in. 'Okay, what happens is, first you get a letter, from Nigeria, addressed to you personally, explaining that . . .'

When finally Stevens had put me in the picture I was at first so sceptical that he got annoyed. He wasn't used to me being anything but his bumbling Watson, his bimbo. I told him he'd fallen for a variation, a new telling of an old joke.

He became so enraged that he walked out on me—this was at the pizza place—and I had to pay. Funny how that works.

The Nigeria Scam involves a letter or, these days, an email, that arrives addressed to you personally, from someone called David Godson, Manager, he says, of the Africa Continental Bank in Lagos. You don't know him but he explains that in 1997 a Mr Barry Kelly made a fixed-term deposit of seventeen million US dollars and then died, leaving no will and without next of kin. If the money remains unclaimed for ten years, the letter says, it will automatically be diverted to the federal government, but if a next-of-kin were to come forward . . . 'I am writing to you,' it goes on, 'because myself as a public servant cannot operate a foreign account or have an account that is more than $1m. Now my proposal is that as a Foreigner, I will present you as Next Of Kin and Partner to the depositor, for the funds to be approved and paid to you. The funds is contained in a sealed trunk box deposited with the security company as photographic materials and family items for export . . . I would not want this letter to get to you as surprised or embarrassement, my intention is to move the funds into your country and invest it in a good business venture, for this reason I want to work with you as artner.' Sic—all of this is sic. 'Should this proposal interest you, kindly call me on 234 8033376024 or send me an email, to enable me to give you more details about this. I have resolved in my mind to give you 15% of the total amount for your assistance. The procedures for handling this transaction is simple, all the documents relating to the depositing of funds including death certificate and an affidavit of claims will be proessed and send to you . . .'

I got all that from a mail that Stevens had printed out and copied for me. Which I now passed to Bernadette. It was a pleasant moment.

*

Say Nigeria and what I get is black and gold. Black, that's the bodies, that's the oil. Gold, flashing on black skin, bangles and earrings, and the flowing gold from the oil. Gold pieces from the slavers (did they get slaves from Nigeria? Couldn't tell you), and oil running, thick and black and sluggish, out of the ground. Then I get the Niger, sliding like a python through tousle-headed jungle, with parrots flashing and swinging monkeys and the dappled spots of the concave-bellied leopard, black and gold and filled with sun.

You can tell I know f.a. about Africa.

But I did know about the Nigeria Scam, from BBC World and the *Guardian* on-line and so forth, it was background knowledge of the current decade. I said this to Stevens, I said, That's the Nigeria Scam, man. I said, Get serious.

By this time we were finally out of the pizza place and had moved, in the pale evening light, to the platz, which is a nearby architectural feature. Mexicoplatz—if you tell a Berliner that you live in Argentinische Allee they always say, 'Ja, bis Mexicoplatz, it was not bombed, that is really schön.' And it's true, the platz is very nice. There's a circle of high old buildings of pale yellow stone and they are topped in brick-coloured tile that is lapped in a regular and highly pleasing manner. The buildings have unusual shapes, a conical one looking like an immense beehive, and the S-Bahn station has a curly façade that is almost cheerful. Yes, that is what I like about the platz, for Germany it goes beyond the merely nice into having character and for once that character is not sombre.

They do so need a nip of the frivolous.

So here we sit on public benches, Stevens and I, and are entertained by the fountain, which Stevens likes because it would muffle what he's saying in case of hidden microphones. 'Of course I know about the funking Nigeria Scam,' he says patiently. 'Aliens from outer darkness with seven pointy heads know about the Nigeria Scam. Give me credit, Rumour.'

He flicks his butt and it flies, an amber arc, into the sparkling waters of the fountain.

'The thing that no one realises about the Nigeria Scam,' he says in an undertone, 'is that it's real.' I am forced to lean in to hear him, which causes a clenching of the stomach muscles. His big black coat should be in the museum of unique odours. 'There really was a guy with seventeen mil. Of course his name wasn't Mr Barry Kelly, but any brickhead can make up a name. The real story is, this guy, whose name I actually do know, did in fact have all this boodle. It's dirty money, blood money, some tribe got the chopper big time, every last body hacked into pieces and fed to the jungle, but that's all history.' Stevens for once was serious—it was as though for once he was talking to himself instead of putting on a show. It was the thought of all those dollars, which were his highway to being A Figure To Be Reckoned With. Instead of just a walking fart-sack.

'Of course, every black man and his black dog tried to get that money. But it's locked up good. Then this wise guy, name of Ido—Mr Abraham Jeem Nineman Ido, how's that for a handle?—he had this sweet little thought: the dosh can't be got, but maybe it can be like a honeypot and attract lots of dopey little bees. He sent off the first scam letter, to a name he got from an American penpal club, and soon he had a nice little trickle of money coming his way. All he needed, this is what he wrote people, was just a few thousand dollars, to procure various documents, pay outstanding legal fees "very minor in their nature". Guy's a legend. He owns half of Lagos. Sitting on his terrace, he looks at the city and goes,

"That one, and that one, and that one—deese all are mine."
All the big buildings. Then he goes, "He he he. De good
Americans."'

Something about this made me stare for a bit into the
fountain. 'You met him?'

'Oh, yeah.'

'In Nigeria?'

'In Lagos, yeah.'

The water in fountains fascinates me. Up it goes, up, up.
Usually there's little jets around the sides, like courtiers, like
jewels around the throat, but it's the central column I'm
interested in—up, up, and then it falls. It's as though it's trying
to get to Heaven. I like watching the highest point, where its
impetus fails and then it folds over and begins its tumbling
descent. It never learns, it's never dismayed or wearied—is the
water all one or should you think of it as droplets, each with
its own identity? After staring at the fountain for a moment I
knew for a fact that Stevens had never set foot in Africa.

The guy breaks a major sweat getting to the dairy for
ciggies. He can't climb onto so much as a bus without
crampons and thirty Sherpas.

But it was supremely pleasant there in the platz, with the
civic grass before us, mown long in the German style, the
blades standing three inches tall in the pale glow of the street
lighting as though, like the water, they had something higher
in mind. The old buildings had the dignity of survivors. To
the right of the S-Bahn station, the wrought-metal bridge
stood blackly in the night air and trains slid back and forth
across it like bubbles in a level. Stevens waited and for once
I made him wait. Like Mr Abraham Ido, if there was such a
person, he had sent his hook out into the world and now was
waiting for a tug on the line. I could feel him, on the bench
beside me, heavy as a safe, the contained weight of him.

'Okay,' I said, 'I'll play your silly game.'

'Ah, Rumour,' he said. And he actually slapped me on the back. It was relief, I think. 'I knew you were my man.'

'And then?'

This was Bernadette, in our night kitchen. Also heavy as a safe.

'He put the bite on me.'

I said this innocently and she took it hook, line and sinker. 'So how much did you give him?'

'Just a couple of thou.'

She gave me a look that could bring on an ice age, then stormed out. But I caught her arm.

She was white with rage, and furious at being held. 'Darling,' I said lightly, 'I didn't give him a penny. Because he didn't ask for any.'

Gough Whitlam, ousted Prime Minister of Australia, once told his people, Maintain your rage, and Bernadette has ever been his disciple. Now she was wild that, at such a time, I would dare to play games with her. She gazed down upon my restraining hand with disdain.

I said, 'He sold his house. How do you think he got here? Air ticket to Berlin, some local travelling—he's cashed up. He's serious.'

'That pig wouldn't know serious if it was his maiden name,' she said. Jerking her arm free, she stalked down the hall into darkness.

But the worst was over.

When, three years ago now, I first came to Berlin, I was surprised by its leafiness. I guess I'd seen *Wings of Desire*

and expected Teutonic buildings, moody, pillars enclouded
and greyly noble. Maybe a few bomb-sites—no, that's dumb,
the war was sixty years ago, but, the sense of bombs having
fallen. Something bleak, maybe—I'd seen some of Kiefer's
blasted landscapes in an exhibition at Shed Eleven. What
else? That's right, I expected it to be chic. It's not chic. It's
more village-like. Okay, with four million people, but in so
many places there's a local atmosphere—small-town locals
buying local-baked bread from their local breadshop. The
dinky superettes—Wellington has miles bigger supermarkets.
Yes, it's the shops, which are mostly little and ordinary. With
little, ordinary customers. That's a bit mean, I guess—there's
something about Germany that makes you feel it's okay to
be mean. What could that be? But there's very little grandeur
here. Not much excitement. People go about the place,
fulfilling functions, achieving the shopping—maybe with a
sense that it might vanish if they don't. How can a place be
so solid and immovable and at the same time harbour an
anxiety that all of this might crumble if we once relax our
grip? If we fail, loudly, to insist that schedules be maintained,
if we don't admonish, grimly, primly, whenever we spot the
tiniest deviation from the rules. Agh, don't get me started.

German
stereo-
types

But then there's the trees. I hadn't expected so many.
And so vigorous. Of course they're all numbered—sorry,
I'm slipping back, aren't I. They're vigorous partly because
they're young. No tree is older than sixty years. The old
trees were all bombed, or caught fire, or were cut down to
make fires when there was no fuel. But the city is thick with
them—chestnuts, with large flat leaves, bigger than your
hand. In the weeks after the slough of winter the buds start to
appear. Then it all happens so quickly. The leaves come and,
I can't say otherwise: they gladden the heart. It's the colour
of them, which is a wonderful primary green, through which

trees

light shines. There's also extra oxygen pumped by them—
is that true? I imagine it to be; anyway, the lungs expand.
And suddenly the bleak streets you have been dragging
yourself down for months, like an ant in a channel, become
a marvellous stroll within a sort of outdoor tunnel, a long,
open room. *lakes*

And lakes. There's thousands of lakes in Berlin, did you
know that, ringed by trees, by woods, that are laced with
paths. How can a city seem so pastoral? I have never been in
a crowd here, in fact, often there seems to be no one about.
And yet it doesn't seem deserted either. This is very pleasant.
To wander quietly, beneath trees, kicking cones, crunching
acorns, and then, going gently downhill, to come to a lake.

The Schlachtensee, for instance. From our place it's ten
minutes by bike and is Bernadette's favourite. She gets us
out of the house—'Where's Fred's water-wings? Where's
Sandy's jellies? Where's Sal? Sally!'—and, after a stop for
croissants, we're away. Sally rides on ahead, doesn't want to
be seen with us, Bernadette follows, Fred and Sandy are in
a two-wheeled chariot that I tow behind the bike, strapped
in, Sandy looking at Fred to make sure it's okay to be here.
Fred is waving at the Germans, who like kids as an idea,
and wave back—as long as they're silent or departing. I once
towed this chariot, in the early days, when we had only Fred
to put in it, through the Brandenburg Gate. The German cars
are good about cyclists, they make room, and so down the
middle of the fast lane I went, between the Gate's soaring
pillars, under the flying pediment, and out into the sunlight
and the Tiergarten: I felt as though I had conquered the city. ✗

At the Schlachtensee, the water looks milky, utterly
peaceful. It's a long lake, with wriggles and loops, set in dense
woods. We find a gap in the trees, get changed on the bank,
take up our traditional roles. This means: Bernadette gets

triumphalism?

quickly into the water and swims out. Sandy looks longingly after her, wails, points out towards the deeps with his pudgy finger extended, thinks about crying uncontrollably, is comforted by me, then deftly palmed off onto Fred. Fred, skinny in tiny blue togs, is busy digging a canal at the muddy water's edge. For the next half-hour Sandy bugs the bejesus out of him, wanting the spade, the bucket, standing in his canal, splashing, shouting, ranting up and down on the shoreline—right through the canal zone—like a demented dictator. Sandy is the most uninhibited of the kids, and to see him running full-tilt, naked, fat tummy ahead of him, one arm up, shouting, as loudly as he can, 'Oi, oi, oi, oi,' well, this is good for the heart. Fred is more or less patient. He is dedicated to his cause, which today seems to be, making a half-circle moat that this bucket will float the entire length of, and only pushes Sandy hard a few times and shouts at him and angrily rips the bucket away and once pushes him so that he falls and I have to move. I towel Sandy down, tickle him a bit, borrow the bucket, 'Just for a minute,' get him splashing in the shallows, then go back to being immobile. I have my book.

Close on either side of us there are trees, which make shade—I hate direct heat or light—and also a kind of frame through which the lake can be viewed, a window to it. Bernadette swims back and forth across this window, in a stylish crawl, or floats on her back, a long way out, where the clouds are reflected.

Which leaves Sally.

Sally is also uninhibited, but in a different way. She undresses, in a bright pocket of sunlight, as slowly as possible. She has taken herself off a little distance, to our left, nearly associated with us, near enough to arrive quickly should the croissants appear but definitely a free agent, a separate nation-state. She has an immense towel, utterly white, and, standing on it, her skin is dramatically brown. She applies coconut oil, slowly, which adds to its lustre. She's naked, of course. Completely, and completely oblivious. Completely absorbed in the slow movement of her hands over her glowing skin, while she moves to some slow, exotic music. Completely, utterly, entirely uninterested in whether every single eye in the area is focused on her.

However, this glowing spectacle does not attract the flies, as it would in New Zealand. Germans are grown-up about bodies—to them, everyone has one. To either side of us, people dress and undress whilst in conversation. Many swim without costumes, wading slowly out to stand thigh-deep, wrinkled bottoms palely reflected in the dark water while they get used to the chill. Alone then in her splendour, Sally finally lies down, throws her arms around her blow-up pillow, and lies, abandoned to the sun.

There's no wind.

Which is just another of the ways in which you know you're not in New Zealand. The still warmth of the air, which is rare down in that long, skinny country. The unmissed sunburn. And the considerateness of the people. There's actually a huge number at this lake today, I would guess three or four thousand, but you'd hardly know it. No boom-boxes, no jet-skis, not even any shouting. This is the good side of German correctness, that people don't feel they have the right to impose themselves. Maybe it's because for a few centuries they have lacked 'living-space', as Hitler put it, have had to live cheek-by-jowl? No drunkenness, no noisy commerce. Most people seek out, as we have done, a place of their own. Not that you can claim it. Everyone always feels free to come right into your little spot and get undressed, bum before your eyes. But with a kind of quiet consideration. Yes, there is a lovely mood of sharing the peace. The Germans have a feeling for peace.

Finally Fred gets sick of being canal-master and comes to kneel right beside me, putting his head down to look, under his fringe, up into my face. 'Dadda. Dadda. Dadda.'

'Fred, darling, you're shivering, put a shirt on.' But these are entirely wasted words.

'Dadda, let's play cards.'

'We haven't got any cards.'

'Yes, we have, I brought some.'

He fetches them from his backpack and, in the lakeside dirt, on the twisted tree roots, I try to lay out a hand of Patience. It's a *Lord of the Rings* pack, with Frodo staring up anxiously at us. The movie was too scary for Fred, ditto *Batman* and *Spiderman*, but he likes the branded merchandise. 'So,' I say, 'a red seven, what's that looking for?' Fred's eyes go over the numbers with extreme slowness.

Now Sandy comes and squats on his heels to watch. His hands are wet and I won't let him hold the pack, so he squeals. I have to tuck him, clammy little body, in between my thighs, where I squeeze him tight so that he is frustrated. But he endures this because he's watching Fred to see what Fred will do. Now Sally comes. Languidly; I can't look at her. She comes round behind me, puts her arms round my neck, rubs herself on my back. 'Sally,' I say, 'go put on some clothes.'

It's a real problem, this. She loves me, and there's palpable affection in everything she does. And I am her one-and-only dad. But it's too much. Kissing goodnight, I have to be careful or I get a tongue-kiss. Her smooching would go on for hours if I let it.

She returns, in her bikini, which wouldn't wrap a sausage, and takes control of Sandy. He lets her. He loves Sally, follows her with his eyes. She mostly ignores him. Then suddenly he's *her* baby, and Bernadette and I can get some peace.

Bernadette comes striding ashore, shaking droplets, white with cold. But radiant—she loves swimming. 'What's this?' She looks down at the cards, which on the tree roots are lying at angles, sliding everywhere. 'Red ten on the black jack,' she says. She wraps a towel around herself. Then she squats beside me. Her hair smells of lake. Putting a wet arm across my shoulders, she kisses my ear.

Little ripples make mouth sounds in the shallows. The family gathers over the cards, intently.

*

Meanwhile, back at the fountain: 'Okay,' Stevens said. 'If you go down Argentinische Allee for one block, there's Sven-Hedin Strasse, to the left. I guess you've been up there.'

This was triumphant, and sly. That he knew my district, knew something about it that I didn't; oh yes, this was an ace up his dirty sleeve.

'There's always a cop car, yeah?'

'Yep,' I said. And it was true, now that he mentioned it, halfway up Sven-Hedin there was often a green-and-white squad car at the curb and, on the footpath, sort of loitering, a cop. Once, I remembered, the cop had stopped me with an upraised hand when I'd been walking Sandy off in the pram. There were gates, which had been open, and a car had turned in. As I remembered it, the car had been nothing special, just your standard suburban box, but the cop had known it was coming. It turned in, the gates swung shut, then the cop waved me on.

'That is the Nigerian Embassy. You didn't know that, did you.'

It wasn't a question.

61

Before us the fountain continued to play in the half-light of the platz. Now there was something maddening about it, it was a thing that kept on, talking like a radio, and wouldn't let you think. Nigerian Embassy—where was Stevens taking this? He made a show of looking to the right and to the left—well, he made a show of everything—then bent and addressed the heel of one of his boots. They were long, rose nearly to his knee, black, and at one time had clearly been superior specimens. They had however the unfortunate effect of making him waddle a little, and he was already a porker. But he wasn't the kind of person you advised on these matters.

He had a keyring and, with what appeared to be a small spike that hung from it, poked into a drill-hole in the heel. The heel turned in his hand, revealing a secret cavity. From it, like a magician producing a handkerchief, he drew a piece of paper and unfolded it.

It was dusty—I imagined the fine dust of the street working its way into the cavity—and gently he shook it. In the night air, dust fell. Magic dust, fairy dust—I was utterly enchanted by this wizard production. He blew on the paper, lightly, as though he was trying to puff something into flame. Then, with a tenderness inspired by true love, he unfolded it on the fat of his thigh. It was a plan—the plan of a building, drawn in pencil. As I leaned in, fascinated, for a look he muttered, 'Just act normal, Rumour.'

'So what should I do, pick my nose?'

He gave me a disciplining glance. 'You want to see this?'

'Oh, come on, Stevens, I don't exactly see the hidden camera.'

Now he looked hurt. But it was show-hurt, he was up to his elbows in bullshit. From inside his coat he produced a photocopy of a map—it was a blow-up of the platz where we were sitting. 'We're here,' he said, and his yellow fingernail tapped, 'the fountain is there. That's where we just ate dinner, and there,' his finger moved an inch to the right, 'is where the camera is.'

Automatically, my head swivelled. 'It's okay to look,' said Stevens smoothly, 'it's not working. That's why we're sitting here.'

He sat in silence. Next to me on the bench I could feel the relaxed stillness of him, so different from his earlier antsyness. Now he was confident. While he waited, I began to reconstruct our evening. I had chosen the restaurant—surely that was true? But maybe he'd known I would choose this one? There were two others, but they were both a lot further away. But our apartment, right here in the district he was interested in, hadn't we chosen that? My mind was like that scene in a movie where they spool back to something that happened earlier and the hero looks as though he's having a revelation.

I became aware that my mouth was hanging open.

Now he was folding his papers. Map back in pocket, plan back in boot. I wanted to study that plan but he was lighting another cigarette. The match lit his features—his nostrils were swollen with satisfaction. He inhaled deeply, then produced a perfect ring of smoke, which hung in the air as though it was his personal logo. He was so proud.

'Okay,' I said, 'I'll be the dummy: how do you know the camera isn't working?'

'Because I cut its cable.'

I frowned at him.

'Last night. About 3am. I used that little tomahawk in your basement.' Again, I was catching flies. I saw him notice and got it closed but he had me reeling. 'A car turned up this morning,' he said, 'about six, to check, but that was just the checkers. Now I've got my clock on the camera techs. They're still not here.'

Right then I wanted to shout: Bernadette! See! I'm not stupid! He's a genius! We're going to be rich!

Instead I stared into the ceaseless climbing of the fountain water and tried to understand what it was telling me.

Chapter Five

'Our next task,' Stevens announced, 'is to retrieve our weapon.'

This was three nights later.

I didn't like that our.

There'd been, in the Lyons/Rumsfield apartment, a kind of bruised truce in operation, with Bernadette prepared not to kill me as long as she never saw Stevens. For his part, he was comfortable with being hated, it'd been his bread-and-butter for years. Sal continued to come and go, as it were, between the two worlds, but Bernadette had her instincts on pink alert and, five minutes after Sal disappeared, would stand on the patio and shout, 'Sal! Phone for you!'

Things were almost normal.

Except that Stevens continued to call on me for Special Assistance. I was to be in on his move—'This is my big move,' he'd say, rubbing his hands—on only a partial basis, out of respect for my hindranced circumstances (children, intelligent wife) and also because of my job, for which I had to maintain outward respectability. This meant that I was only to be involved whenever he thought it really necessary, which was all the time. This limited availability meant that my share of the payday would of course be reduced.

However, wrestle me to the ground, the payday wasn't actually the big thing for me. Oh, I like free money as well as the next guy; and if it meant we really could afford to finance an extension to our progeny department, well, that would keep Bernadette sweet for, oh, three years easy. But if, in the privacy of my own company, I stare into the mirror, what I get is a voice that says, You're going under.

Listen: I read recently that Americans on average have between four and eight holiday days a year. Well, thank you, America.

The *Guardian* recently had a piece about this schoolteacher in Birmingham fired for talking in his humorous blog about 'my evil boss'.

At the Memorial every personal phone call results in a warning memo from the Administration.

Did you know that when you sign on at Wal-Mart they have an aptitude test. If you answer 'Disagree' to 'There is room in every organisation for a nonconformist' you fail. It has to be 'Totally disagree'. I read this recently: if you answer 'Agree' to 'Rules have to be followed to the letter at all times,' you're wrong. It has to be 'Very Strongly Agree'. And something inside me felt its jaw begin to jut. I mean, I'm no rebel. But Wal-Mart is the world's leading organisation, top of the *Fortune* Five Hundred—where they go we follow. Aren't we all rather climbing into a concrete suit these days? Any colour you like as long as it's corporate. Any justification you like as long as it plays on the market.

Listen to me: sometimes a man's gotta take a walk out in the night.

So it came to pass that after dark, and inspired by a couple of cans of Warsteiner, Stevens and I turned right out of my gate, passed beneath the camera (now repaired), and made our way *up* Argentinische Allee, *away* from the side street with the bridge, and our gun—which was our target for the night. Stevens said the camera was nothing to worry about, it was focused along Sven-Hedin Strasse, where there were two embassies, and didn't care about dogs that pissed down at the foot of its lamppost. Along then past Café Krone, all closed up until morning, right at the Berliner Bank, along past the driving school where, glancing in, students of the steering wheel could be seen sitting in a semicircle, earnestly learning to drive whilst indoors. Now here were the houses. This part of Berlin has front lawns and personal gardens. The houses all look as though Miss Havisham might be in residence, with high, gabled peaks and small windows at a variety of levels which suggest a profusion of small and interesting rooms. The people who own these houses are wealthy. But they aren't chic. There's the odd style-car, one Maserati I've seen, two Ferraris, but mostly its just upscale suburban round here—the kind of environs that makes me want to be a renegade with a long coat and a sawn-off shotgun. Oh how I'd love to step out of their DVD players.

But their wealth buys them silence. The streets are cobblestone, the trees are like friendly presences, presiding, leaning in to shed leaves and acorns through which the wealthy feet happily crunch. Stevens and I don't talk. This is slumberland, this is where you come so that your brain can die in peace. But it is very pleasant.

Right at Goethestrasse (we also have Schillerstrasse and Kantstrasse), which is parallel to Argentinische Allee. We were now on the other side of the little lake, the Waldsee, which is at the bottom of our garden. Here, let's have a map, I love a map.

affluent area

slumberland

lake

Is slumberland the new Berlin? Silent area.

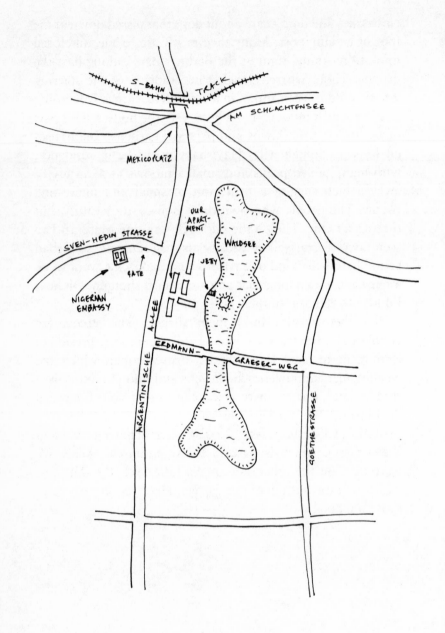

S-BAHN TRACK

AM SCHLACHTENSEE

MEXICOPLATZ

OUR APARTMENT

WALDSEE

SVEN-HEDIN STRASSE

GATE

JETTY

NIGERIAN EMBASSY

ARGENTINISCHE ALLEE

ERDMANN-GRAESER-WEG

GOETHE STRASSE

68

Stevens reasoned that the dog which had necessitated him loosing a bullet had come from the Argentinische Allee-end of the little street, Erdmann-Graeser-Weg, which ran down towards the Waldsee-Brücke. A brücke is a bridge, a weg is a way, a strasse is a street, well, you knew that last one, but I slip it in out of solidarity with those of you who, like me, have never acquired another language. Okay, and to get this over with, wald means wood—doesn't wald have a lovely old ye-walds-of-Englande feel about it—and so we lived near the wood-sea, which is just about right for this sweet, sleepy, leaf-mouldy, tree-thick neighbourhood; sniff up that rich pong.

And Stevens and me stomping through it like yokels.

We turned into the little weg and there was the brücke. Glancing back, I saw that there was the spot where, three nights earlier, the Polizei had entertained us in the back of their van. My heart began to bang. Okay, yes, I admit it, I was feeling a little worried about this particular walk in the dark.

But Stevens was all passionate unconcern. Professionally, he assessed the situation. 'The light falls onto the bridge,' he said, 'from the lamp up at the far end, so anybody looking down here from *that* end of the street has to look past the light—they won't see much. Also up there,' he pointed, but with his hand down alongside his hip, so that any observer wouldn't notice, 'are the bushes where the Hound of the fucking Baskervilles was hiding. So we won't be going up there. Whereas from this end,' he massaged his chin so as to indicate deep thought, 'there's no light, so anyone coming from *this* end will see clearly what's happening on the bridge. Okay. So I'll stop here, make like I'm looking for something that I've dropped, and hold up anyone that comes this way. So you'll have a clear shot at getting the gun.'

Me?

'It's between the third and fourth stanchions after the third main upright,' he said, 'right hand side.'

'Right hand side—really? Thanks. I was here when we stashed it, remember?'

'You wouldn't remember your thumb if it was up your bum, Random. Get going—and walk quietly.'

Stevens genuinely liked these escapades. Me, I liked them in hindsight. I was sweating as, practically on tiptoes, I advanced along the bridge. But, really, there was nothing to get hung about. It was a beautiful night, calm and still. The bridge was pedestrians-only and thus didn't have strong lights to brightly drive under. Instead, the old lamps had been retained. This is a side of Germany I like, the way that they don't madly modernise everything. These lamps had four small glowing points that burned like the mantles of the Tilley lanterns my dad tenderly applied a match to at our bach, they gave a soft, gassy light. Trees grew from the banks of the lake, down below, so that as you approached the bridge you were up among their cloud-like tops. The bridge itself stood in the night, with air below it, air above, air all around it cool and moist from the lake. No, this was a lovely scene and as I walked into it I made like I had just come out of a romantic movie and had symphonies in my head.

At the third upright I paused, as though suddenly attracted by the sight of the Waldsee, faintly rippling below. I sank to my knees as though deeply moved. I pressed my head to the bars as though my passionate desire was to get closer to all that boundless nature. My hand went between the bars and began to feel around. Nothing. All nonchalance, my fingers explored.

But I wasn't feeling nonchalant. This was a mission with a high risk of failure—if suddenly I bumped the gun it would fall from its narrow ledge and then Stevens would demand that we drained the entire lake—inconspicuously, of course. Also an issue was the way my fingers had to be in a place I couldn't see. What if there was a fucking great spider? Or an earwig or even an ant—I don't like wildlife running on my body. And then: Aha!

As my fingers described the shape of the butt—the gun felt cold, serious—there was a cough from Stevens's end of the bridge. Was that a warning? I loosened my hold and relaxed, returning to rustic-poet mode. I was about to ease my head back from the bars for a glance his way when, without warning, a sound came, this time from the other direction. It was the sound of hooves, fast and getting faster. Something big, really big, was coming up from my left. No, it wasn't hooves exactly, that was the echo of the bridge—just as I was figuring this, a terrible sound occurred, right behind me. It was a savage bark.

Instinctively I trust away and therefore made a perfect job of jamming my head between the bars.

Now footsteps approached, slowly, like Mr Plod the pleeceman. This was Stevens. He hissed, 'Fucking dog. Piss off, dog. Gowan, piss off. Oh, never mind then.'

What did that mean?

It meant that the dog, having scared the wits out of me, was now completely happy and entirely relaxed—two nice men to play with, one of them even down at dog level. Thus it came alongside me, chummily pressed its flank against mine, then put its head through the next-door bars and inclined its muzzle so that its long tongue, glistening in the evening light, could lay a generous streak of slobber on my cheek. Meanwhile my knees were being rasped by the knobbly surface of the bridge and my head felt as though a migraine-shaped peg had, on either temple, been whacked in by a mallet.

Plus my bum was stuck up in the air—Stevens said, 'Get the gun, Rumour, or I'll be forced to arse-fuck you.'

'I'm stuck.'

'What?'

'My fucking head is stuck.' Also, I was forced to look down. Below me, the water looked like something in a Tolkien movie, a living, thinking presence. I had this feeling that it was drawing me forward, encouraging me to fall. I am not crazy about dark water. When I was nine I was in a river in the northern Wairarapa, going down for the third time when a hand came out of the sky and pulled me clear. I can still remember the surface being above my head, the way it wobbled and flexed up there, something unattainable, like Heaven. Bubbles everywhere, too beautiful. My lungs filling, the water pouring down my throat as though it had a will to invade. The solid volume of the water, everywhere, all around me like a filled room. And that white hand which came out of the sky.

Then I heard more footsteps, Stevens saying, 'Evening, officer. Um, um, guten Abend, mine Herr. Mine Freund ist, what's the Germanic for *stuck*, Rumour?'

'Fertig.'

'Yeah, that's it: Mine Freund ist Fertig, Ja.'

How we do like to master a foreign tongue. Fertig means finished. But dummkopf Stevens didn't know that. He didn't know Arthur from Martha, if he was a toothbrush or a broom. But he was talking his head off, gesticulating wildly no doubt—I couldn't see anything except the water below, which was calling to me—walking in noisy circles as he raved. 'Ja, Ja, da Kopf vor mine Freund Fertig ist, Ja, absolutement Fertig ist.' I heard small clinking sounds and instantly knew what they were: handcuffs. They were going to handcuff me to the bridge! Shoes shuffled immediately behind me. Then there was a yelp—someone stood on the dog's tail. The dog bit my backside.

It was just a nip, it never broke the skin, but I didn't know that till later—I yowled. This set the dog off and there were terrible sounds, growling, shuffling, shouting, scuffling, maddened voices. What I was certain of then was that someone was going to kick me. All I could hear were feet, the sound of shoes in agitation, and in my mind it was clear that every one of those feet had an impulse in it, a yearning. How can you see a bum in the air and not want to go for the goalposts? Someone was going to lose control.

The water said to me, Come, come, you will be safe with me, come, it's so very quiet down here.

The dog licked my face again. The handcuffs clinked. The shoes scuffed and scratched. The voices made no sense. The migraine pegs went deeper. The water called my name. Finally there was an accidental moment of silence and into it I threw my voice—if I could have thrown my head back I would have, but instead my whole being came out of my mouth: into the night I howled, 'Bitte! Bitte! Bitte!'

'Why didn't you say so in the first place,' said one of the cops, and he bent over me, Schwarzeneggered the bars apart and I was free.

I sat on the bridge, head down, blinking.

Having once taken this position it became hard to look up. I couldn't do it. I couldn't care. I sat there like a drunk-in-charge and waited to see what would become of me. I didn't thank the policeman. I didn't thank the woman who pulled me from the river, either. I just ran off along the riverbank, wanting to get away. Back in the world.

'Ja, Ja, gut, ja, gut.' That was Stevens. 'Danke schön, Ja, Danke. Danke. Das is gut, Ja. Ja, Danke.'

'Shut the fuck up,' I said to the pavement.

But I was wrong, again. The cops were laughing, Stevens was laughing. Ha bloody ha, it was all a huge joke.

It wasn't true, about the cop saying, Why didn't you say so. It was just some German, but that's what it sounded like. Everything was a subjective impression—it felt like the dog had given me a life-threatening bite, it felt like I'd been knee-capped, it felt like there were headache pegs driven so far into my head that they were meeting in the middle.

But I was free. We were free to go. It was all a big laugh. And off we went, Stevens and I, accompanied by the mother-loving dog, who trotted happily beside us and then as we passed them, nipped into the dark bushes to await the next instalment of *Carry On Up The Brücke*. When, at Argentinische Allee, we looked back, the cops were there, on the bridge, watching us. We waved, and they waved back.

Next day, on my way to work, I deviated to the bridge, bent down, retrieved the goddamned gun and stuck it in my backpack.

I suppose I should say something about my job.

When two-and-a-half years ago we arrived here I was in a state of total gobsmackedness at being asked to come. Germany! Berlin! The edge! On the coat-tails of my NZ boss I rode the globe to edge-city Berlin and we got the Memorial going. This is the Memorial to the Murdered Jews of Europe, designed by famous US architect Peter Eisenmann (I hadn't heard of him either) and standing in Berlin as a stagnant field of mud for years—sorry, that should of course be, as a memorial-in-progress. My boss is, as you may know, Project-Manager-To-The-Stars Kelly Grantly, who for years has been getting stuck-in-the-mud cultural projects like the Museum of Australia up and running. Kelly is a genius and I am not fit to wipe the sweat from his Excel sheets. But he does, as he occasionally half-admits, have one slightly less-than-genius area, which is communication. He is a great talker, brilliant. But just every now and then people are unclear about what it was he might have said. Yes. Which is where I come in, apparently. To tell the truth I was amazed that he chose me to bring. But people say, You and Kelly go together like coffee and a cup—the stuff you're after is there, but something has to stop it from all draining away. That's a quote, actually, from a smartmouth at the head office, but I think it makes Kelly sound ineffective, which is so not true. However, I do know that I can always explain to people what it is specifically that he wants them to do. 'And get them to do it,' he says, giving me a wink. It must be true or would I be here? Pinch me.

Whatever: here is where I am.

And so is the Memorial, which amazingly will open to the public in May. A field of concrete stele, thousands of them, each one immense, long (like a coffin—but you aren't supposed to say that), and between them walking paths, so that you go down in among them, feeling them rise around you, each one just slightly tilted, like old gravestones (or that either)—the feeling is of being immersed in the death of six million people. Right there in the middle of the city, with city traffic going past and slotted views of the Brandenburg Gate and the Reichstag, glorious, except that from down in the middle of the Memorial they don't look quite the same. Check it out on www.denkmal-fuer-die-ermordeten-juden-europas.org—it's extraordinary.

One of the things you can't help stubbing your toe on in Germany is the Holocaust. Literally: in the street where we first lived in Kreuzberg there are bronze cobblestones each one of which records the name of a Jew who lived in the house adjacent and their subsequent fate: 'Died in Riga.' When at Wittenbergplatz you emerge from the U-Bahn to shop at KaDeWe there are hoardings and directional signs and then there in the visual mix an almost flimsy-looking placard which neatly lists all the camps that trains from this station once departed for—Auschwitz, Bergen-Belsen, Treblinka, about a dozen of them. These things shock by being just quietly there in the fabric. For grand gestures there's the astonishing zigzag museum of Daniel Libeskind, which is more like a sculpture than a building, but for me the most powerful things are the ones you stumble over and have to give a second glance to.

But the Memorial is amazing, amazing. I'm very proud.

And then one day when finally it was all in go-mode and Kelly and I were starting to feel we could let out a breath, I was called into the project office's conference room when the Stiftungsrat, which is the Memorial's board, was in session. I'd been warned, I was wearing a good shirt, but, my understanding was, I should say a few words about the need for a range of safety measures I'd written a report on—handrails, anti-slip treads on the stairs, etc. There were about twenty of them, all men, all older, including Kelly, who, when I entered didn't for once meet my eye. The boardroom has an oblong of tables with an open space in the middle, it's weird, you study everyone's ankles. There was a lot of cigarette smoke—this is Germany—and at least two of them were smoking cigars; from the density of the fug I'd say they had been going for days. So I sat in the empty chair, opposite the chairman, and waited. There was some heavy talk in German, which I didn't try to follow, and then apparently a decision was taken.

Now the chairman, Herr Professor Doktor Wildt, exhaled

a blue cloud of smoke and then put his head forward into it. Completely enwreathed, he felt comfortable, and so he began to speak. 'Herr Rumsfield,' he said evenly, 'the Stiftungsrat is happy that you agree to stay on at the Memorial. This is good.' Around the table there was nodding. 'Ja. Your contribution has been completely good. We are grateful and have every wish for your happy future. Ja.' More nodding. I nodded back, modestly. 'But sometimes we cannot always act as we wish. Sometimes we cannot act alone. As you know.' I felt a little tremor start up in my knees. I looked for Kelly and found that now he was holding my eye, somewhat soberly. 'Your director informs us that you have been good effective.' More nodding, and long, satisfied exhalations of blue smoke. 'Too effective. Is that possible to say? Herr Rumsfield, you have been too good effective, and this is what the problem is, for us. I do not think this will be a problem for you.'

So why was everybody so goddamned reflective?

'You have been I think to Sachsenhausen.' This wasn't a question, he obviously knew—I'd been on an official visit with Kelly when we first arrived, and again privately. Sachsenhausen is the site of a concentration camp, an hour north of Berlin. Now an image of it came into my mind: a flat, burned piece of land, triangle-shaped, immense, with broken buildings, edged by grey stone walls with gun towers. Grim. Every step you took there was heavy with the past.

As this picture opened in my head I understood that they were sending me there.

Trying to send me—I just wasn't going to go! It was an extreme prospect, a place like that with ovens—a shooting gallery that had nothing to do with needles, a lab that had no test-tubes—that someone might try and *make* you go there. But the chairman was still speaking.

'We would wish to keep you here,' he went on, 'but unfortunately this is not possible. Of course, when the procedure there is complete, of course, naturally, then you would return.'

I drew myself up a little and said, 'I have a contract.'

Kelly fixed the chairman with a contractual eye and nodded. But I know Kelly Grantly, I've worked with him now for yonks. The eye was for show. Kelly's lovely open face told me plainly, I'm a bad actor.

The fix was in.

At my mention of the contract, everyone pursed their lips, as though this had been anticipated. 'This is true, Herr Rumsfield. But it is not a simple situation. This contract is with the approval of the Arbeitsamt,' the work permits office, 'and they have suggested that now the development phase of the Memorial is over, that we have no right to continue to retain you. This is not our wish. This is a matter for regret on our side, Herr Rumsfield.'

Now he waved his hand in front of his face so that for a second the smoke cleared. He looked at me frankly. 'I do not think, Martin, that the Arbeitsamt came to this conclusion all by themselves.'

I glanced around the room for allies. Our Geschäftsführer, the head of our administration, a grandfatherly man who had always been an enthusiastic supporter of mine, was holding his gaze steady on the square of carpet down in the middle of the tables. Now I saw that, under his silvery moustache, his teeth were in his lower lip.

'What exactly is being proposed?'

Smiles broke out: I had accepted. I wanted to go, Whoa, hold on!

'The situation is this. That place is a place of trouble. When you learn more of its history you will understand. For many years the intelligent portion of the Bund has wished to develop it also as a memorial.'

'But it *is* a memorial,' I said. I clearly remembered buying a ticket at a ticket office.

'Yes,' nodded the chairman. I saw now a kind of grimness in his face, and that this was also in the faces around the table. Grimness, and a kind of embarrassment. Germans facing their history in front of an ausländer. 'But the memorial is to the victims. But outside the grounds of the work camp, there is another piece of land, with buildings. This you will not have seen.' I didn't know what he was talking about. 'These were the offices of the administration of the camps. Not just that camp. Sachsenhausen was the first of the modern concentration camps built in this country. It was the model. And all the other camps were administered from there. Not the death camps, that was another place.' Everyone sucked in their breath at this, as though it was a relief, as though it had been a close one. 'Do you know how many of these camps there were, Martin?'

I shook my head.

'In Germany, over six hundred. And that one was the centre. So. The intelligent portion of this country wishes to extend the memorial so as to take in the site of the former administration. To acknowledge the part the administration played.'

He said this with such upright formality, with a stiffness about the jaw that indicated strong self-control. I do have great respect for these high old Germans, who force themselves to speak of the terrible thing that rose from within their culture. I understood that he was himself an administrator and that there was, in his mind, a line of responsibility that went back. 'But the townspeople don't want this. They don't want their town, the town of Oranienberg, to become famous for that.

So: for many years this land and these buildings have been there, in the possession of the nation, and they are ghosts. Some say they should be pulled down, burned, and new things built. Ja. Others say they can never be removed. It is an impasse. No one can agree and nothing happens. It has been observed, Martin, that you are an expert at getting people to agree. Ja, in some very high places this is known.' And now the room seemed to swell with a weird pride—that one of their own had been recognised, was that it? But I was swelling with something else entirely. 'And so this Stiftungsrat has been asked to release you so that you will be able to— what is this word you are good at?'

'Suffer?'

'Nein, not suffer,' and this made him irritated. Angry, even —that I would indulge my feelings when Germany's shame was in the room. He turned to his colleague and muttered a question. Then he said to me, 'Facilitate. That is it. That is what you do, Herr Rumsfield. You good efficient at . . .' he conjugated, 'facilitation, Ja, und so that is the situation.'

'No,' I said firmly and shook my head.

That is what I emphasised later, telling it to Bernadette. 'I told them, No, and I shook my head. I was utterly vehement.'

'And what did they say?'

'The old man said, I do not think it is possible, that you say no. For the Stiftungsrat, that is not possible. As you know, he said, Berlin is in a difficult circumstance right now—'

'Five billion euro in the red,' I said to him. I shouldn't have said this, it was rude, but I was angry.

'As you say, mein Herr, five billion euro in the red ink, and this affects the position of the Stiftungsrat. Also, Deutschland itself is having some . . . difficulties. As you know. This means our funding might be cut. But those institutions which can show they are doing good-positive things and are not over-spending, well, they will be protected. Also, those institutions which co-operate . . .'

'I'm not moving out there,' said Bernadette.

We were in the kitchen, as usual, our boxing ring, where all the big stuff gets knocked about. 'That's what I said,' I said, 'I said, I am not moving my family out there. And they said, That is fine, Herr Rumsfield, there is a train from Potsdamer Platz, this takes only forty-five minutes.'

'So I don't see what the big problem is,' Bernadette said, and she moved to make herself a new pot of tea.

So that's my job.

I have, I know, a soft idea of humanity in me, that formed through the benign years of my growing up in New Zealand. This set solid the year that *Sgt. Pepper* came out, when I was fourteen. That year's radio song was *All You Need Is Love*, which you can't like these days, it's like liking the national anthem, I can't bear to hear it. But maybe that's because it once meant so much? The idea that it will be possible, once we get things right, for humans to be kind and happy and for life to be a sort of never-ending party—you should be killed for even having allowed yourself to think that, but, at that time—please hear me on this. At that time it genuinely seemed a possibility. And with me it was personal. I know everyone moved on—there was decadence, and then punk, and then greed and then there didn't seem to be any point in tracing the impulse any longer. But, me, I stayed with that childish belief—it was childish, and ignorant—that the world could be a nice place. I think it's fear. Of what you have to know, and still carry on. Of who you have to be. People think we old hippies are just too smoked out to bother with keeping up. But it's fear.

And now Sachsenhausen. Did I really have to face it?

81

Chapter Six

One night I head down to the keller only to find Sal there alone. Stretched out on a red leather couch, she has her chin on her fists and is looking steadily into a dark corner of the room.

I should describe this couch, it's such a monster. Bernadette, who is an habitué of junk shops, found it at the back of an op in Kreuzberg and got their muscle guys to lump it up four flights of stairs to our then front room. It's the colour of old blood, with a high arched back and a skirt round its feet which is kind of dainty. Three flat cushions, stumpy little arms. The leather is studded with black-domed nails, between which it bulges as though its cheeks are puffed out. It belongs in the waiting room of some evil dentist—did I mention uncomfortable?

But amid the assembly of street-person accessories gathered by Stevens—dead-thing sleeping bag, death-throes pillow—it stands now up against the wall of the keller as though it has drawn back in horror.

Stretched out on it, Sal heard me coming, I know she did, I came down the ladder for christ sakes, which is maybe two strides away. But she continues to stare down as though she is deep in the most profound kind of inner debate. I decide to wait this out and stand, hands behind my back, in the middle of the subterranean room.

She's getting tall, Sal, taller than Bernadette, but willowy. Dark curls, it's lovely hair, actually—both Briar and I have nice hair. When I was in my late teens I had hair that fell halfway down my back and once, years later, Mrs Bewley, who lived across the road, said to my mother, 'What ever happened to Martin? He always had such lovely hair, that boy. I used to sit across the road and I would always say to Len, Hasn't Martin Rumsfield got lovely hair, Len.' My mother passed this on so that I would have something positive to cling to in moments when I was thinking of killing myself. Briar's hair is curly and mine straight and, who knows how this works, but Sally has finished up with a really magnificent tumble of dark, wavy hair which she flings around to dramatic effect, and hides behind, and chews, and hits you with, and threatens every day to cut—this is a kind of suicide threat—but never does. Her complexion is good, though I predict trouble. She is willing her breasts to grow so hard that pimples just have to erupt, through a kind of outlet-needed kind of thing. Cheekbones, a straight nose, maybe a little pinched, a pleasing brow, though on its way to being prematurely lined—she frowns. She's no beauty. Bernadette said this to her once: 'You're not beautiful, Sal. You're pretty and you're attractive and if you don't ruin yourself lots of boys will run after you. But beauty is about character. It's not a thing you can see in a mirror, it's what you see on the outside when someone is beautiful inside.' Thank you, Bernadette. Oh, I know what she was trying to do, and Sal's relationship with mirrors is the reason we've missed a thousand trains. But I had Sal on my knee that night for two hours, sobbing. 'I'm so not beautiful. She's right, I'm just not. Bernadette is right about everything, I'm so pig-ugly I should wear a bag over my head. I'm going to live in one of those places where women hide their faces behind a blanket. I'll have to be a lesbian. I'm breaking every mirror in this house, right now—let go of me!' Etc. Bernadette is hard on her, partly because Sal is hell to live with. But only partly. The real reason is, I know, because she disapproves of Briar—

everyone disapproves of Briar—and doesn't want there to be a Briar-stain on her kids.

Our kids.

In some ways, that's not fair, Bernadette does think of Sal as hers and would fight for her and is always kind to her, in her way. Sal adores Bernadette, she worships her. But this is a sad love because Sal knows that Bernadette can never really, deeply, finally, love her back the way she loves the boys.

She loves me best. Sal, I mean—the best in the whole world. It's an honour to be loved like that.

And—I admit it—a burden. Of course I love Sal. Of course I do. But it's a strange love, all mixed up with my disapproval of my worst self, which was obsessed by Briar. I see Briar in Sal and I am afraid. When we find a needle in her bedroom or she brings home some crimo gang thug for a boyfriend I am going to be revealed for all the world to see as a pathetic creature. See, see—see that? It's all about me. I do know that, and I hate myself for it, and resolve to do better. But then when my eye falls on Sal, somehow I just can't make myself concentrate.

Having her feet up on one arm of the couch means that her spine is bent like a bow—how can that be comfortable? But it's kind of dramatic and she knows it. She lets a week go past, and I wait this out. Finally she turns her head (huge flick of hair) and says, 'Dadda, do you think that having an older boyfriend is okay?'

This is so daytime-soap transparent that with a sigh I sink to the floor.

As I said, we had an old purple carpet that we put down here—now it's thick with ash, and also other things that I don't want to look at too closely. What with the old-cigarette pong and the pizza-box pong and the crouching smell of mould, you really do need alcohol to spend time down here.

But I make myself. When a Sal-and-Dad moment occurs, I can feel myself trying to summons special reserve forces. I have Bernadette in my head, saying, 'Be hard on her, it's for her own good.' And I know what she means. But I feel guilty. I feel I should forgive her as I forgive myself—neither of us really coming up to the higher standards of the civilised world. And if this is anyone's fault then it's mine, all mine. I feel that I owe her.

All of this in our exchanges.

'Sal,' I say to the river of hair, 'Sal, darling, listen.' But what am I going to say, really? That Stevens is a terrible person and I should never have brought him into our lives? He's a filthy user, don't believe a word he says? Instead my mouth opens and turds begin to fill the air. 'You know, Sal, when I was your age I met a girl, well, she was a woman really, I guess she was as old as Bernadette—'

'Really old,' says Sal.

'Shut up. Anyway, she seemed to me to be everything that I wasn't—sophisticated, experienced,' I search for a Sal word, 'cool. And she kissed me once, at a picnic—'

'What was her name?'

Unmarried kissing: I understand that I now have Sal's total attention. 'Helen. Helen, ah, Fields. She was like you, she had lovely hair.' Sal sits up, puts her chin in her hands, and gazes at me unblinkingly. It's weird this, their fascination with your past, Fred is always asking for stories about 'when you were a boy, Dadda'. He listens in total silence, you can hear his mind working, then says, 'Tell it again.' They seem to find it amazing that you were once like them, small and finding your way in the world. Of course, there's also the fabulous charm of the olden days, when you had to outwit fierce bulls that had treed you or made carts out of apple boxes that went speeding down terrifically steep hills—when was the last time you were in the presence of an apple box? I sound like grandfather time—that's what I get for having my kids late. My but the weather was golden back then.

'Did she really kiss you?'

'Yes.'

'Was she really like me?'

'Yes, quite a lot, actually.'

This makes Sal completely happy. Eyes the size of planets, she sits with an entranced smile on her face, willing me to go on. Standing now on the purple carpet, I pace, one hand moving in the air as I talk. 'We were out at this place called Double Bridges, there's a river, I nearly drowned there once, anyway, that's another story. So this Helen Fields was a woman that my mother knew, though she wasn't quite as old as my mother—'

'Grandma Margaret.'

'Yes, Grandma Margaret, and her teatowel blew away, miles, it was really windy, and I ran and got it. I had to climb a fence, there were some fierce steers, but I got it and brought it back to her,' suddenly I can see all this clearly, 'and Mum and Dad were sort of round behind the car, where our picnic was, and she had her picnic on a blanket, down beside a lovely pool—'

'Was she by herself?'

'Yes, and—'

'How come?'

'I don't know, perhaps she was a bit unhappy or something, anyway, I gave her the teatowel and she said, Thank you Martin. And then she put her arms around me and kissed me.'

'On the mouth?'

'Yes.'

'Did she press her body all against you?'

'Ah, no, no—but I could feel this kiss on my forehead, like it was burning—'

'You said on the mouth.'

'No, it was on the forehead.'

'That's different from on the mouth.' And a certain look comes onto her face. Suddenly she isn't so interested, and a terrible thought comes into my mind—that Stevens has kissed her: on the mouth. Now I have another picture, this one has water in it too, the water of our lake, and there are trees and the jetty, and down under those trees bloody Stevens . . .

'Anyway,' she said, 'what happened?'

'Well,' I say, 'then I was convinced that we were in love. And I sat around the house with all this love in my heart, and I thought of her loving me, from inside her house—she lived two streets away—walking around in her rooms and thinking about me, beaming something towards me, and I felt a kind of singing all over inside me.' I can't look at Sal. Not when I'm trying so hard to kill something that's part of her. 'And I . . . had a special song on my record player that I used to play, that I knew she would—'

'You said you never had a record player until you were sixteen,' Sal says crossly—this from an old argument about when she would have one, which definitely was going to be way before sixteen. And she leans back, puts her arms up behind her head and arches her spine, as though she's pushing her body away from a heavy dream.

'That's true, but Mum and Dad had one and there was this record by Frank Sinatra—'

'He's definitive cool,' says Sal.

When she says it it sounds like coal. But how can it be that she likes him? I don't even like Sinatra, not that much. But my dad did. He had this one LP, *Where Are You?*, which I used to play. 'And I would play that and think of her. Over and over—I used to sing it under my breath. And I wrote her a little poem. And I read things in books that I thought she would like, if I read them to her.'

'So and?' says Sal—she's guessed what is coming.

'Well, darling—what do you think? She was a grown woman, I was a kid. I was in lala-land. I was just dreaming. She didn't know I existed.' But then I decide I have to crunch this home. 'I was really sure. I completely believed that she was interested in me. And d'you know what?'

I wait, but Sal's gaze has wandered. I realise that she is looking up in the direction of the window through which Stevens will eventually return. 'And d'you know what?'

She puffs out a huge sigh. I feel like I'm torturing her. But I have to. I say, 'I lost a whole year of my life. For a whole year I mooned around the place, staring at the door, thinking that at any moment she might come through it. Grandma Margaret thought I was sick, she took me to the doctor. And d'you know what? It turned out that actually she had a *daughter*, who was just my age, and I'd never even noticed! And one day this girl, Frances, well, Frances and I, we—well, never mind.'

'Da-ad!'

'What?'

At which point there *is* a sound outside the window. Sal's face tilts upward, full of hope. But it's Bernadette. She puts her head in, screws up her face—that'll be the pong. She puts her hand over her mouth. 'It's nine-thirty,' she says.

'So and?'

'Don't be so bloody rude, Sal,' I say. 'Go on.'

Bernadette's eyes go from me to Sal, then back again. I give the smallest of nods. Now Bernadette is looking steadily at Sal, and something grim is forming around her mouth. She is just about to speak. But then she thinks better of it.

This is because Sally, on the couch, is sitting upright, smiling to herself as though the existence of something previously made of mist and hope has now become a solid object, a thing you could kick with your foot but that would only make it be there harder. Sal tilts her head forward and disappears behind her circle of hair. While Bernadette and I exchange meaningful glances, Sal has a private moment, the reverie of a queen who is thinking of subtle and pleasant things that lie several days' ride away. Then she rises and calmly makes her way to the ladder. All uprightness, she climbs.

For the first time in recent history, Sal agrees that it's bedtime without a fight.

The map in Stevens's shoe, when finally it was unfolded before my eyes a second time, turned out to be an object both mystical and dull. There were no words on it, only the floor plan of a building, just rooms and corridors drawn in pencil. In this it was like the plan of our Kreuzberg apartment I'd drawn for Mum and Dad and mailed off as part of trying to give them a sense of where we were living; something mundane and domestic. But there was a number written on it, 232/B, this was in a corridor, at the point where there appeared to be a door, and it had a double underscore, for important. The door gave into a room; in the room were oblongs, which I guessed were desks, seen from above. And inside one of the oblongs, along at the right-hand end, was a small but distinct 'x'.

As in, X marks the spot.

I tilted the map to the light to get a better look, but the only light available was coming from a match held by Stevens. It was late, we were on the bench-seat down by the lake, the

Waldsee, near the little jetty where, once, in another time, I had blown bubbles with the kids, before running up through the rain. The silence of the lake was now a low, waiting thing, as I held the map, which seemed to have been drawn on tissue paper. My fingers pressed hard against my thumbs so that, even if something unexpected happened, it wouldn't be torn away. Then Stevens moved the match, down behind the paper and, before I realised it, up from below. The flame expanded—in my hands, the paper caught fire.

Frantically, I flapped the pieces, trying to put them out. The bit in my left hand burned me and I dropped it. Carefully Stevens picked it up and angled it so that it burned completely. It glowed, then crumpled—for a hot second the pencil lines on it could be seen, ash-white suddenly against the now black background. It was utterly flimsy, a butterfly thing—this was the last time it would ever be seen. The number written on it glowed but I just couldn't make it out. The paper began to break up and he let it. There was no detectable breeze but nevertheless it floated, crackling in the night air, out over the silent water, and was gone.

His forefinger tapped his temple to show where the plan was now. Unfortunately this is also the gesture used when someone has a brick upstairs, to use it on yourself is sort of incriminating, but Stevens has no feeling for negative details, the beer cans of life feel free always to spray him upon opening as they know he doesn't mind. In fact he had an open can in his hand which had done this, his beard was foam-flecked and dripping, but his monologue came forth undaunted. I'll spare you and summarise. Mentioning again the now mythical figures of Roger and Diana and Preed, he gave a disconnected and dissatisfying account of how the map came into his hands—from this I gathered that he'd more or less stolen it—and then began to free-associate on something referred to as 'the next phase,' in which we would go to the 'x' and recover the object that was there.

'What d'you think it is?' I asked.

In the night, the trees leaned in to catch his answer.

'I *know* what it is.'

'Going to tell us?'

He had finished his can and, apparently absent-mindedly, started upon mine. I didn't care, it was warm. He made me wait while he chugged. Then he uttered a loud belch, in the silence the sound went out across the water and, in their little nests, tiny birdies shivered. 'Ah, Rumour,' he said, 'it's like the plan, see, information needs to be kept where it can't escape. Right now, you don't need to know.'

'For my own good.'

'Exactly.'

'In case I get captured and tortured.'

'You think everything's a game, Rumour.'

'It is a game. Hundred thousand dead Iraqis, what's that but a fascinating game?'

'Don't start on that toss. This is not a fucking game. When you get your hands on a suitcase full of big ones, then you can give all the speeches you like. Until then, we maintain discipline.'

Even the trees saluted.

Torture—now there's a word that without warning had come back into everyday speech. I can't remember when previously I spoke it, it used to be an Amnesty International word, a word for things that happened in other countries, in dirty places far away. Suddenly now it was on the news, our news, every night—our guys had tortured. Our team—the white guys. Could have been me.

Yeah, I know, there's something ridiculous about that—once you start down that road, everything just spirals inwards and before you know it you're confessing that you once cheated in a spelling test in standard two, shoot me now. But there's something about the way the world has gone since 9/11 that instantly means everything goes to extremes. It's like something has been loosed, everything's up for grabs and the big grabbers are really going for it. This US election seems like the ultimate battle between good and evil—I heard Spike Lee on the BBC the other day saying, 'Seems like the upcoming presidential run-off is not gonna be important for the direction of the United States, it's gonna be important for the direction of the world.' Which was what I'd been thinking, but when you hear it said. It made me feel I was nineteen again and thinking that if Nixon won the possible world would come down in flames. Now I'm walking through Charlottenburg with Bernadette and the kids, on the way to some newly opened spielplatz, and there's a giant billboard for one of the newspapers, the *Morgenpost*. It covers the entire wall of a building and is divided in half. On one side, JFK's face, immense, and the words *HIER spricht ein Berliner*. The other has my namesake, the loveable Donald Rumsfeld and the words attached to him are, *DA spricht ein Amerikaner*. This thing is the size of a skyscraper, it's like a fucking wall of truth, and I find it kind of maddening to look upon. 'See! See!' I say to Bernadette, and borrow a pen from her to write the words down.

Standing in the street, scribbling down words from a billboard while we are getting late for our train—she gives me a very sobering glance.

But it's everywhere. Listen, I can't even watch the sports. The Olympics are on and to tell you the truth I have never much cared for the Olympics, I just can't get off on running or throwing or synchronised pig-wrestling. But then I see, sitting there semi-glazed, that this has got an angle. That there's Americans in everything and I can be against them. Instantly I'm getting so that every time an American wins, I grind my teeth. Isn't there something prancing about them? I read on the *Guardian* site that they were told not to flaunt their triumphs, because it might increase hate—if this is not flaunting, I am the Hitler of modesty.

I decide I can't see *Fahrenheit 9/11*, it will only make me crazy.

Crazier.

You know, I tell Bernadette I'm in with Stevens for the money. But it's not the money—I know there'll never be any money. It's just that I can't bear the thought of who I am if I say no to him.

The straight way, these days it's so crooked. What was it Bob Dylan said: To live outside the law you must be honest. All right-thinking people instinctively know this to be true.

But what if I screw up? What if this whole thing with Stevens is putting my family at risk? What am I doing here— half a belly full of beer, sweaty round the neck, bored actually, worried, superior somehow to Stevens yet playing the tail to his comet. Sitting on the bench alongside him, within the pong zone. Nodding. Listening when he speaks: I ought to be committed.

'Okay, this is the plan,' he said.

'What if I get given a truth serum?'

'Good point, no, you're right.' And he folded his arms and held his face like a mask.

The lakeside trees begging to be in on the secret. 'Oh, come on,' I said.

His eyes slid to the left side of his head, which was nearest to me, like marbles rolling in a jar. His look was sceptical, withering. I tried to find the right face with which to make a response—subservient? Enthusiastic? Serious?—but the eyes continued to find the idiot in me.

Then, with the sigh of one forced to bear a terrible burden, he began. And thus the plan was finally spoken.

'Today week,' he said, 'it's a Thursday, at twenty-one hundred hours, we leave from here. Wear dark clothes, nothing you can't be seen in, nothing that will attract attention, but dark. No alcohol all day, and don't come home late. I want your house settled and running as usual.'

'What's my house got to do with it?'

'Nothing, nothing, I just want you to concentrate on your job.'

'Promise me nothing will happen here.'

'Nothing. There's absolutely nothing happening here, I promise.'

Now the eyes were as dead as the gaze of a fish on your cutting board. In the head behind the eyes, no music played, no birds sang. It was a wasteland, an empty land. Downslope from us there on the bench lay the lake, a weight upon the earth, a container for the undersuck of trouble, that pulled like gravity. There was a message here, if I could only grasp it. Stevens saw that he had to set the hook. Oh, he has an instinct for your worst self—he plays that like it's a pinball machine. Now he said, 'Of course, a big-time project man like yourself obviously has to know how all the eyes get dotted and the tees get crossed—am I right?' Clearly I wasn't lighting up bright enough. 'Because you're pretty corporate these days, aren't you, Rumour. I'm impressed,' he said. 'I never thought you'd get set so solid.'

He was filling me with gloom and he knew it. 'So what's next for you?' he said, 'Iraq? Gitmo, maybe?'

'What?'

'Well, I'm just following the line,' he said reasonably. 'You're in the memorial business, the atrocity business—there's always atrocities. I guess you're set for life.' He lifted his beer can, made what might have been a toast.

I had the sense that my heart had been fed something that both sped it up and slowed it at the same time.

'Anyway, I guess if I'm going to hold the attention of someone of your calibre,' he said, 'I do have to trust you with the odd fact.'

He gave me a long, measuring glance. I had a hand to my chest, feeling for palpitations—it gave me, I imagine a patriotic, a sincere look. It all felt okay. After a moment I gave what I guess was a nod. He took it as a nod. He nodded back.

And that was all it took.

'Okay,' he said, 'this is the goods.' He paused, brewing a little resentment that he was having to give over. 'Remember I told you that the Nigeria Scam was the real deal? It's been worked for years and old Ido, he's like the Nigeria Scam king. You want to see his place, Rumour—women in solid-gold underwear—'

'Sounds comfortable.'

'—diamonds heaped in the sugar bowls. He has his coffee brought on a little wagon pulled by a team of frogs. Little gold harnesses, looks great against the green of the frogs. And the trainer of frogs just stands there, smiling confidently—they never spill a drop.'

I stared at him. Stevens has the imagination of a root vegetable. So where'd he get all this from?

'Now Ido's essentially retired. But all these years he's been plugging away at the original lolly that got the whole scheme started. He bought Preed—remember him? Preed got his cock jammed in one of Abraham's fuck-holes, had to sign himself over to get out. Guy's essentially lost his identity. Abraham had him working on the problem of the original lolly—"de mudder-stone", Abraham calls it. It's there, in a sealed box, and no one can touch it. "I gots to have it," says Abraham, "for reasons of sentiment. Ha, ha, ha."' Stevens doing Ido's laugh was like the cawing of the deadest crow you ever heard, every plant for miles around was withered. 'Okay, Preed thought, Where can I go? Where's far enough? And, you know, one of the main virtues of the Land of the Long White Smoke Machine is that it's way down there on the bottom of the map. Where he got entangled with Diana— remember Diana?—and the rest is history.'

He set aside his can with a satisfied finality.

I waited. I could hear the sound of the lake, little warning noises.

'That's it?' I said.

He sighed like a man who is sorely tried. Now I got the eye again. 'Are you in, Rumour?'

'You know I'm in.' I said this disgustedly, but he didn't mind. Stevens faces disgust in every mirror.

'Preed's cock,' said Stevens, 'is just an arrow for ruin. Diana got him. He should never have gone in there. Couldn't help himself.' Now he let out a huge sigh of satisfaction. 'And I had Diana.' Now he really did make a toast. I gave another of my might-have-been-a-nod's. 'She owed me. But she had Preed. So I got Preed. And Preed gave me Abraham.'

'Meaning?'

'Preed gave me the map, set me up with Abraham, and Bob's yr uncle. We go in, get whatever's at the X and we're the jolly kings of lolly.'

'In the Nigerian Embassy?'

'Yep.'

'We're going to break in?'

96

'We're going to make a surgical incision, remove something that no one knows is there, that no one will miss—like taking out a pancreas.'

'And then?'

'The item at the X,' he said, 'instructions maybe, a password, whatever—that is what will get us to whatever opens the strong-box with the original boodle. Which will be jointly handled by Abraham and myself. And, bingo, we're drowning in champagne.'

I tried to find an objection to this but there were too many to choose from. My mind was like an empty nightclub, the sense that things had previously happened here was overwhelming. Later that night as I lay in our bed I tried to have a thought, any thought, on any given subject, but nothing would come. All I could get were pictures of myself with Stevens and we were sneaking somewhere—sneaking as in crashing loudly beneath big neon that read, We're criminal fuckwits, come laugh at us for free. The other thing that occasionally came through were the big ones. Yes, intermittently they were there, glowing as though radioactive. But I couldn't get them to go together with the fuckwits.

I slept as though I had somehow slipped into the lake and was being pulled under.

Meanwhile the war in Iraq. What was it Donovan sang? 'And the war drags on.'

Yes, meanwhile the world on TV, cheer yourself up with the breaking news. George W talking of 'the freedom of the Iraqi people'. Meanwhile liberation, which is just another word that has Orwell's tongue in its ear. Meanwhile the election, which it looks as though I am going to lose. Fred beside me on the couch and Sandy beside Fred as we watch CNN—two small faces looking up into mine. 'Dadda, why did that man go on fire?'

Meanwhile my terrible face in the mirror, that I can't bear to look at. I catch it sometimes and then in the moment that follows try to see what was there, the meaning, before I adjusted it. I look like I am wishing I could be arrested.

Chapter Seven

Then something happened.

In a marriage, what seem to be events are only symptoms, the actual events are long, stretched-out things, deep buried like strata. The ground shifts, but not suddenly; it only feels that way.

It happened at the dining table, as is proper in domestic life. It went like this.

I was wandering through from the shower, towel around, still in the just-got-home daze, with Fred dancing round me going, 'Dadda, Dadda, look, Dadda!' and Sandy biting my ankles, when my eye fell on something. It was slim, it was lying on the table, keeping a low profile, just something left there. Just angled so as to accidentally catch any passing eye. It was a literary magazine.

You know the kind of thing, slim, never mentioned by your friends, or by anybody, ever, actually. Circulation of seventeen, held together by chewing gum and love. This one was from Wellington, New Zealand, its name was familiar as Bernadette occasionally bought a copy: *Sport*, which is not a name I've ever understood but lots of these things are in-jokes. In fact it looked rather professional, with one of those obscurely interesting photographs on the front—a dog carrying a beer can.

And so I picked it up. Geoff Cochrane publishes in *Sport*—looking for him, my eye went down the contents page. And there it was. *Bernadette Lyons, Three poems.*

She wrote when I met her, you know. When I first was allowed to visit her flat, there were scraps of paper, not exactly lying around but you would occasionally find something folded small and tucked under the sugar bowl, jotted while doing the dishes, wet fingers making the letters run. I remember that flat, with its walls the green of pea-soup—nauseating. I remember a holiday on Waiheke, when she dragged me out of the sack early and made me go down to swim before anyone was about. It's funny: for one so puritanical, she is remarkably fond of swimming without clothes. I remember her standing thigh-deep against an on-coming wave, and the early light coming off the rounded shoulder of water and how it made her eyes look greener. I saw her—I don't mean the sexiness of her, though that was part of it, but her form, the musculature as she braced herself for the wave. The lovely thing that she was—how, I thought, could I ever get her to love me?

That was seven years ago, and since we have lived under the same roof I have never, once, found a single scrap of paper with those higgledy, twitched lines of little letters on it. Whenever I have mentioned poetry to her she gives me her sourest face and makes like she doesn't know what I am talking about.

And now this.

Because, you know, I thought I had killed it in her. It's the thing you fear the most, I think, to be responsible for the decline of another. That they didn't become their best. It's the parenting fear, that little Johnny, instead of pursuing his obvious talent for brilliantly mimicking birdcalls will, because of some disparaging remark of yours, go on to become a highly competent banker. Not that I want my kids to be brilliant, that is one of the very few things I suspect I am not guilty of, but interested, in their own lives. Bored people, it's a crime against nature.

Here's the one poem.

How for example the sight of him
Producing two perfect
   poached eggs
Every sequential Saturday which makes him so happy
Will keep you able
To breakfast at the same table.

Okay, the other poems were better, even I could see that. But *they* weren't about us. About me. But she had offered this one anyway—a kind of public announcement, an advertisement even, that could be used against her on Judgement Day and might be read by those members of her family who felt I wasn't good enough for her.

Funny how you sometimes think of the things you will bring to mind when you realise you have only ninety seconds left to live.

Meanwhile Sally shouting in the night, a rising clamour: 'No. No. No! No! NO!' Awoken, I ran down the dark hall, feeling vulnerable because I didn't have any pyjamas on. I burst into her room. But she was sleeping, it was only a nightmare.

Meanwhile Sachsenhausen, which was like a swamp I kept tiptoeing round the edge of.

On the Monday I came home and there was a little fashion parade. This happens from time to time. Bernadette had found a flea that sold kids' clothes and Fred and then Sandy came through from the hall, did a turn, received my applause, then ran back to Mummy's arms. Bob der Baumeister teeshirts, a shirt with an elephant on the back that Sandy insisted on wearing the wrong way round so that he could see it, various trousers and shorts of no great distinction. Bernadette had even found herself a skirt, which I really made a fuss of.

Then Sally piped up: 'Now it's my turn.'

Bernadette looked at me and I gave the slightest I-dunno shake of my head. Sal had shot off down the hall. There was a wait long enough to bake a pizza, during which Fred disappeared with Sandy to bounce on our bed and Bernadette and I resumed our usual state of feigned hostility (insurance against the real hostility). I still had it in mind that the poem might change things, I could feel a kind of goofy smile in my chest that was just dying to rise to my face, but one look at Bernadette and I was saying to myself, Don't be silly. I had just poured her more wine when someone came into the room.

I have to say there genuinely was a half-second when I didn't recognise Sally. Spike-heeled boots that made her taller; hair up; fake glasses with heavy black frames that gave her an air of gravitas and chic; a long black leather coat that went in and then out. Under the coat, more or less nothing. A micro-skirt, also in black leather. And, above, a thing that I think is called a bustier, which gave her remarkable breasts— stuffed, of course, but they looked plump and promising. Plum lipstick—she looked like a starlet playing a hooker.

I was slow but in a flash Bernadette was up out of her chair and in Sally's face. 'Get that off! Where did you get this?'

Sally attempted a twirl but Bernadette gripped her arm, jerking her so that, from the height of her spikes, she was in danger of falling.

'He bought them for me.'

Stevens had become a name that couldn't be uttered. Now Bernadette turned to me and gave me ten burning yards of her anger. Eyes in mine, she said to Sally, 'Get all that off and bring it to Martin, who knows what he can do with it. Then get your face washed.'

It's strange to see your daughter taking a sexual shape, I found it disturbing. But, I won't deny, part of me was struck by the possibilities. Now, now, calm down, it's okay—I don't have a problem. That would be something I never wanted to come close to. But it's not hard for me to see that other men wouldn't feel this way. And that's it. To see her suddenly as other men might see her, it makes you terrified and proud and angry all at once. I sat back on the couch during this female bust-up, blinking, thinking. Bemused. Nodded at everything Bernadette said—yes, yes, of course, dear. But somehow in elemental shock.

The presence of the future.

Sally had gone off down the hall—too easily, I thought— she was planning to fight another day. Which left the two of us on the couches, me blinking and brow-beaten, Bernadette not prepared to look at me. The air was singed.

Finally she said, grimly, 'You think he can just hang at the edge of things and it won't affect us.'

'I'll ask him to go.'

'Tell him!'

'Okay, I'll tell him.'

'Give him those . . . things! And tell him to bury them. I never want to see her looking like that again in my life.' She sighed. 'Martin, this is so bad for us, living here.'

'I'm working on it, darling,' I said. 'In a couple of days, I'll have the whole situation totally deloused. Just give me a couple of days. I'm going to bring home the bacon. And this I promise: then you can have another baby.'

'On a clear day,' she said, 'you can see the promised land.'

*

103

Later, when I descended to the keller, I was carrying a bundle. Sal had, under Bernadette's watchful eye, passed everything over—wrapped in a swaddling of tissue paper. The lipstick was gone and her hair had been taken down; she was just a girl again. But her back was to Bernadette when she passed the bundle to me and she looked into my eyes with a look of utter complicity, as though she knew I had seen something that, from now on, couldn't be denied. I couldn't return this look, indeed I didn't really know what it heralded, but I duly noted it.

Yes, I duly noted everything, the way you note the nails they are going to drive through your wrists and ankles.

It was the order of the day: I saw Stevens note my face as I placed the rustling parcel on the floor near his feet. He was figuring what this meant, but I couldn't help him as I didn't understand. He wasn't really interested in Sally, I knew that. Then why? He leaned back on the red couch and blew a logo of smoke towards the ceiling—I could feel Bernadette, up through one layer of floor, watching down with her x-ray vision. I was kind of struck dumb, I didn't exactly know how to act, and so I sat on the carpet, frowning. Finally Stevens said, 'That's all of it?' I nodded—I presumed so. He nodded back, slowly. He massaged his chin, then sighed. I could see that he wasn't discombobulated by this latest development, indeed, he seemed to have expected it.

That was on the Monday.

On the Tuesday I turned up at work in pyjamas.

It's humiliating, I know, for a man my age to allow his wife to buy him his clothes. But she says that I dress myself like I'm angling for a pension and that she has to look at me. The truth is, she likes buying things and if she's buying for me then she's not spending on herself, is her argument. Also—and I do see this—it's a gesture of affection.

She is extremely alert to gestures of affection, Bernadette. They embarrass her and she ruthlessly prevents them from leaking, like acid, into our lives. It's part I think of a hyper-alertness to cliché. Oh, and she wants to be able to leave me without people saying, You seemed so happy together.

Unfortunately at present her taste seems to run to stripes, stripes, or how do you feel about stripes? She says stripes are hip and who am I to argue? Thus I find myself, having dressed in the first shirt off the rank, sitting in an incredibly serious meeting, in Sachsenhausen, in the offices of the former Inspector of Concentration Camps, in the company of Sachsenhausen's leading historian and other historical men of equally distinguished character, and I'm dressed like a joke Arab who has been dragged in from central casting.

But somehow this is appropriate, somehow it works. Of course the shirt is untucked, it's like—I said it—pyjamas, and of course everyone clocks it, and frowns. But if I am to have any effect in this job, it will only be a result of never, ever fitting in. I have to be the grit in the oyster, I see that—the cuckoo which lays the golden egg.

I attempt to take the meeting seriously.

The celebrated deconstructionist architect Daniel Libes-kind once addressed the problem of Sachsenhausen. It was he who stirred up the trouble which today, and for every day of the last fifteen years, has been frowned over by the men in this room—and by Frau Gruzdz, who represents, she says, the citizens of Oranienberg, the small town in which or near to which or some distance from—this is all contested—the concentration camp stands. To me, there is no place where the town ends and the camp starts, they run into each other. But, after the war, the town's citizens, when taken to the camp, said they had no idea that it was there.

Frau Gruzdz took to hanging signs on her fence which said, 'Don't let them put a stain on our town' and 'Oranienberg is not Sachsenhausen'.

This was because Daniel Libeskind, a Jew many of whose family were murdered by the Nazis, had declared it was 'an historical impropriety' to, as the city proposed, tear down the offices of the former Concentration Camp administration and replace them with residential housing (millions queuing to live *there*, I'll bet, but that was the plan). He was taking part, in 1983, in an architectural competition to design the housing, but, deconstructing like anything, he refused to accept the limitations of the brief and instead exposed, expanded, exploded the proposal, saying that, yes, buildings in which civic functions were carried out might well be built—never housing—yes, there was no reason why the site shouldn't become useful, productive. But it had to be done in such a way that the past was not obliterated; that it was immoral and dangerous to tear down the past; it had to be lived with; lived amongst. Thank you, Daniel: the jury thanked him, gave him a special award to recognise the rightness of his thinking, and told him to go away. But Libeskind, who is high-minded and tenacious, refused to do as he was told and began a personal campaign, which lasted through most of the decade he lived in Berlin, to have his proposal accepted. He and his staff went, in Oranienberg, into pubs with butcher paper and plans, they attended local meetings and spoke passionately. And Daniel Libeskind is one hell of a talker—I have seen him often on TV, and then up close at the Memorial. He's diminutive, about five nothing, your classic leaping gnome, and has a fat-cheeked, babyish face, from which his gappy teeth protrude in a semi-circle, like a mouthful of tacks. When he talks there's a danger of spittle. But the words are a torrent. They're visionary, close to William Blake at times, with reference to angels and our higher selves. He uses the word 'we' to describe the human species. He puts himself in his frame in the most uncompromising and inspirational manner. By these means, he connects, especially with those who are not as well educated as he is. Listening to him, you feel—I feel—a huge desire to be a better person, to read those hard books, to live on an elevated plane amid buildings both meaningful and spectacular.

I never saw him in the pubs, that was before my time.

Gradually he induced a crisis. His ideas took root in that portion of the Oranienberg breast which wishes to grow oak, to be as pure as nature. Some of the locals began to take his proposals seriously.

But. The former administration site is now used by the German police as a training ground for recruits (who presumably are dead to history. I mean, don't they feel weird learning to police *there*?). The police academy want to totally reshape the site, tear down everything, build new facilities, a sports track, a gymnasium, up its capacity. If Libeskind's plan gains ground, none of that will be possible. The police will move their training facility, and the money that flows from it to the town, elsewhere.

The office we are sitting in is now occupied by Herr Kappe (that's Herr Professor Doktor Doktor Kappe—I kid you not), who is Official Historian of the Historical Site and Director of the Sachsenhausen Memorial. His first name is Uwe, which you say *Oover*, and I can never hear this name without grinning at the vacuum suck of it. A tall, jowly, fleshy

107

man, he's from the Ruhrgebiet in the north, an industrial district known for producing wry pragmatists, hard-headed iconoclasts. He wears a houndstooth jacket and, underneath, a black turtleneck instead of a tie—what a rebel! And I mean it. In the culture industry you stick to the uniform. His belly is vast but he carries it well.

When I first came to this office I asked him, 'What was this?' He didn't understand. 'This here,' I said, 'was this a store room? Was it a room for records?'

'Ah,' he said. 'This was an office. It was the office of the former Inspector of Camps. The Inspectorate of all the Camps in Germany was here, in this building, and in these other buildings, and in this actual office is where the Chief Inspector of Camps was working. Yes.'

He sat back in his chair at the end of the table, looking into a hole in the air, the pale fingers of his big hands interleaved on his belly. He was highly tolerant of me. I didn't blame him—I didn't have the faintest clue what it was intended that I might do in Sachsenhausen. I said, 'So how does it feel? To be working here?'

His amused eyes went slowly over my face. Then he said, 'I do not understand.'

My translator had a go.

'Ah,' he said. 'How does it feel to work in the former office, within the same walls, to look out the same windows, and to administer the same grounds as the former perpetrators, that is your question?' I nodded. He gave a shrug that was close to dismissive. 'I am a historian, Herr Rumsfield. My job is to deal with the facts. To know what were the facts.' He looked to see how this went with me.

'But what are your feelings?'

He laughed. 'I am a historian. I do not have feelings.'

I gazed around at the walls, which, these days, were

blandly panelled with polished veneer, books in alphabetical order. Maybe I did this a little pointedly?

I had first come, as I said, to Sachsenhausen as a tourist. You get on a train, blink at the fields speeding past, a bit of a walk through the town (Oranienberg) and you're there. This was Bernadette and me and the kids, with a New Zealand history buff, Hamish Street, who was the friend of a friend and said we should, it was just half an hour up the road—so we did. Sometimes you don't think.

I've been back often, but you never forget the first time. On that occasion I had not the faintest clue what I was seeing. I had expected, I guess, to go to a place where people were gassed in their millions and when told, no, this was 'only a work camp', I was disappointed. Forgive me—at least a hundred thousand died there. Then there was the history. After the war, Sachsenhausen fell under the rule of the Russians and they made it over according to ideology—tore buildings down, put new ones up, erected memorial sculptures. Then the East Germans had a go—more demolition, more building, new memorials. After which the Wall fell and the West had its turn. So what you're looking at is layer upon layer, like some sort of above-ground archaeology. But you don't get that, not until it has all been carefully explained. You see high concrete fences with gun towers and you think you understand.

We wandered into one building, a reconstructed barracks—one picture of twig bodies in a pile was enough for Bernadette to come to her senses. She took the kids off outside the walls and stayed there.

Hamish the history took control of me. He tried to explain. But I had images in my head from books and films, I was sure I understood already. We wandered, I was sort of in a daze—a history daze, where on one hand you are looking to fit what you're seeing with what you've read, and at the same time, saying, under your breath, thousands were murdered here. Feel it—*feel it!* There were barracks, but they had been rebuilt—the original camp oven had been razed to the ground, but I didn't know that, then. In one place there was a high roof, like a giant carport, over what a sign said were the remains of the ovens. You stared at them and saw the books and the films. Later, I learned that I had misunderstood everything my eyes fell on. Then, at the end of a deep earth trench, a real shooting gallery with real bullet holes—now that was more like it.

If that sounds as though I was relishing death well that is true. I had come full of dread, with a sense of obligation. And when I was there: you want to get your jollies.

In every direction the ground was flat, which made you feel exposed under the sky. The earth seemed to have been burned, the grass trampled, everything flattened. Low buildings. Inside them the walls carry photographs, blown up, huge grainy black-and-white things that have images too terrible to be really looked at, and maps, too complex, and tired objects, small mean things that can't speak. None of this was what you had in mind.

Hamish was talking, telling me facts, he wouldn't shut up. But I couldn't fit anything together. That is a guard house. That is a gun tower. Coils of rusty barb. Burned soil. It was a nothing day, as we crunched on the gravel paths the open sky above us was patchy, a broken thing that didn't hold any messages.

We walked and walked, crunch, crunch. Grim buildings, paths—these I could cope with. Inside, I was holding myself. I was still afraid of what I would have to see. There were a few other people, quiet groups, families, and I began to wonder about them. I am a tourist but these people are Germans: what are they feeling?

110

Near the end was a cottage—this apparently was genuine. Not pretty, also grim, but nevertheless well-kept. A neat sign with black letters told me in English that this was the Pathology building, where medical experiments were conducted. As we entered I could feel what I was holding inside saying, Getting closer now.

On either side of the short entrance hall, two offices, open doors with a chain to keep you back but you could peer in. Desks, blotters, ink-wells, everything very neat. On each desk, a skull.

Ahead, a larger room, in the middle of which were two oblong tables, white, at waist height, about the size of doors—about the right size if you wanted to lie down. The white was from glazed tiles, which rose to a rim around the edge, and there were drain-holes so that the blood could run away. In cabinets around the walls were scissors and knives and clippers and saws. They were arranged in arcs, from large to small, as though someone had wanted to make of them a nice display.

Being careful not to approach anything too quickly in case of what you might see.

To one side was an opening and this was the chute where they put the bodies down after they had finished with them. Beside the chute was a set of stairs and you could go below. Hamish said, 'There's nothing much down there,' but I went anyway, maybe just to get away from him. Old narrow wooden stairs, with hollowed treads. Holding myself; alone with myself now. In the dim light underground there was, to the left, a ramp that went up to the world, wide enough to take the carts—one cart remained, old, wooden, high-sided—filled with bodies, and body parts, up and away to the crematoria; there was a pitchfork to speed the process. But apparently they didn't take them immediately, as, turning to the right and going deeper, head ducked so I wouldn't accidentally touch anything, there was a space, cool, expanding round corners, into an underground set of rooms where the bodies were kept. Rooms which opened into other rooms, and pillars to hold the roof away—you were afraid of what might be behind the pillars but they were just bare concrete rooms. I was going to say empty, but they weren't empty. I made myself go in. It was old concrete, rough-textured, and I grasped that it had been washed many times. Washed and scrubbed. I can't tell you what I smelled, I have no idea whether what I smelled was really there—soap, carbolic maybe. And flesh. Inside me what I was holding said that this was it. Someone had walked here, carrying humans, shifting them. Someone had loaded them—pitchforked them. It was a larder, of kinds, for keeping. And it had kept, and would always keep, and when you went there what you got you kept whether you wanted it or not.

Chapter Eight

Getting home after a day at Sachsenhausen always made me want a kiss on entry from Bernadette, a kiss from the kids— Sandy like a thing from a cartoon, his whole body elongated up so that his lips came pointing towards you. Pressing Fred against my thighs, just a moment longer than he was comfortable with. That old song (the sixties again, sorry): 'See me, feel me, touch me, heal me.'

The temptation to riff off here on The Who, who once were my all-time favourites, is overwhelming (never mind that poor old Pete Townsend turned out to be a maybe- paedophile—just play *Baba O'Riley* loud enough and it's all teenage wasteland), but I have been making an heroic effort in the last few years to find music by people born after my glory days. When I got home on the Tuesday Bernadette was playing something finger-popping by the Flying Wonders that I bought after hearing it in a little one-man record shop, a fabulous obscurity that I am completely proud of, and with that as a soundtrack I tried to shake off the day.

After dinner, Bernadette and Fred took to playing tennis- ball-whack on the path outside with Sandy as ball-boy. I watched them from the bedroom window. Sandy clad in just a plastic nappy, his tummy out, knees out, running full tilt up the path, one chubby arm in the air with the ball held triumphant like the Olympic flame—this is better than anything shown on TV ever.

I got onto the bed, put my book on the floor, and looked down on the print. One of the few advantages of getting older is that you get long-sighted. I took my shirt off, lay down, and sighed.

I was maybe ten pages to the good when Sally drifted in. 'Hi, Sal,' I said and kept determinedly on. You know how the kids always think that if you're reading you're not doing anything. She watched out the window for a bit. I saw her bare feet start to leave the room—gold-painted toenails—but she got caught by the big mirror. I concentrated down, quietly turned the pages. After a while it became okay, Sal there staring at herself, not moving, and the kids and Bernadette outside, and my book, and the sound of a low wind in the leaves. I sank deep into the black type. I could have been anywhere.

'Dad, d'you think . . .'

There was a long pause. I kept my head down, sometimes she stays at the mirror for hours, chewing the ends of her hair, making eyes at herself. It's normal, I guess. I didn't look.

Silence. Sandy shouting. I kept going.

A fly or some summer insect landed on my back and I shivered to get it off. Sally saw this and she came and stood over me, waving the fly away. I could feel the faintest puff of air on my lower back, it was pleasantly cooling. I made a little grunt of appreciation. But I kept going.

I felt a finger make a slow circle in the middle of my back. There's a large wart there, it looks like a little cauliflower, it's probably very ugly but I never see it and hardly remember that it's there. The kids are interested in it. They poke it; Fred once drew a circle around it with a felt pen. The kids feel that your body is something they too have dominion over, something they have shares in. Fred plays with the hairs on my chest while I'm watching TV. Sandy grabs any nearby bit of you when he needs to haul himself up. They bounce on you, measure you. You're the dad, the dad-thing, the dad

114

part of their system of living. They own you. It's impossible to imagine ever being separated from them.

Sally's finger shifts and she touches my upper arm. 'D'you still like your tattoo?'

I suppress a sigh. I know what's coming.

'If I had a tattoo,' she says. Ah, this is more interesting, and in the mirror she sees my eyes lift from the page. Seeing that she has my attention makes her think. Her finger is resting on the point of my shoulder, I can feel the thinking going through her. 'D'you think I should get one?' she says.

'What would you put, Sal?'

She makes a small sound, a noise in the throat, and I can tell she's torn between telling me something that will keep me interested in her, or keeping it inside, the power of me not knowing. While I'm listening she moves. She gets up onto the bed and lies down, full-length, on my back.

I shut my eyes—that's the end of reading.

She's remarkably heavy, a solid object with the gravity of the world inside. I can feel her hair all over my shoulders, the moving mass of it. I have mixed feelings about hair, I am always afraid it will get in my mouth and drown me. I check that it's okay, for us to be lying like this. It seems to be. What it feels like is that Sal has finally got me where she wants me, on my own and can't get away. So I keep my eyes shut and wait to see what she'll make of it.

She seems to be smelling my hair. I am faintly repulsed by this but it's her nose. Then she says, 'Tell me why you got your tattoo.'

On my arm, a neat line of inky letters saying, *I coulda been a contender.*

This is a chestnut, Sal has asked for this story so many times that I feel like saying, You tell me. As I said, the kids can't hear enough about your past.

115

'Okay,' I say. 'So you had just been born and Briar said that I should go and get a tattoo, to mark the day. She said I should put her name but as you know, darling, Briar and I weren't, I mean, I've told you this, we weren't together at that time so I thought that that might be a bit funny, so I just decided to put something about how I felt about her.'

There was, as usual, a very long silence while this was again mulled over. Once, at this point, Sally had asked, 'Why didn't you put my name?' and I found it hard to come up with a happy answer. Since then she has not asked that. Now she says, 'What does it mean again?'

'It's out of a film, darling, an oldie, called *On The Waterfront*. There's a boxer who gets beaten up, I think maybe his fingers are broken, and he's lying there all bashed and he says what's written there and it means, I could have had a crack at, you know, fighting for the title.'

Lots of thinking. Then she says, 'I think I'm going to see that film so I can understand.'

I don't want to take this anywhere so I lie doggo. She lifts herself, I can feel the print of her body coming away from mine. Outside, the sound of the tennis ball and Sandy refusing to give it.

Now I can feel the point of her chin digging into the top of my spine. It's unpleasant but I feel she's literally making a point, and I let her. Something about her past. She works away at hurting me for a bit and then switches to kissing the spot, tenderly, which is worse. I am starting to think that it might be time for me to lose patience with this when she says, 'Tell me again about when you came to see me when I was just born.'

*

116

That was the Tuesday.

Wednesday, Thursday, these were just days—you get up and you do them. I had at every moment that trickling sense of sand running, of time running out, but a day is a day, you are inside them like the weather, they're always there and all you're doing is using up another one. Same as with your life—plenty more where that came from.

Coming home Thursday night on the S-Bahn, a bird got into our carriage and dashed its body at the windows. It made your heart flutter.

Kissing the kids, deleting the spam, half a beer, this was the evening order and I dutifully worked my way through it, trying to just do what I always did. Of Stevens there was no sign. I had told Bernadette that by the end of the week he would be gone. An email had blipped into my in-box at work, from an internet café: 'rumour: the bridge at twenty-one hundred. bring your brain.' From time to time I vaguely tried to remember what his instructions had been. No alcohol—well, I had already blown that, but what's a half between husband and wife? Wear black. Yes, and there was something about the house—that's right, nothing would be happening at our house. Well, and it looked as though this was true, nothing was. The kids were complaining as usual about the end of TV, Bernadette was wearing her floppy old house dress, with a million flowers, Sal was quietly applying fresh gold leaf to her nails. I noticed that the Israelis were once again loving up their neighbours, that the Iraqis were continuing to express their gratitude to their liberators. You know, the Germans could tell these people about what a regime that goes all the way can achieve if it sets its mind to it. There are days when I would like to export Sachsenhausen— drop it down somewhere, oh, in Texas maybe, they think big there. Nothing about New Zealand; there is never anything about New Zealand. Oh: cloudy in Wellington. Must write to Mum.

When I emerged from the bedroom in my art-opening clothes, Bernadette said, 'Where are you going?'

'Tonight's the night.'

'At the opera?'

'He said wear dark and this is the only dark I've got.'

The scorn that always rose in Bernadette's face at any unmention of his name was for once tempered by a look of concern—that I was really going to do something with him. This shift was the omen I carried with me out of the house. I went, as he had recommended, away from my destination—around the block. My effort to act normal was being so successful that I really thought I was off on a summer stroll—passing Café Krone, I was tempted by the thought of a sunset beer. Well, it was still warm. My feet crunched the small cones which lay thickly on the footpath; about the size of eggs, they fall from trees called Kiefer. The cones themselves are called 'zapfen', which is a nice word. As I crunched through the zapfen it occurred to me that maybe this wasn't the smartest time of year to be going out on a sneak-mission—I presumed that was what this was. Acorns and leaves and zapfen made, now that I listened out for it, every footfall sound like a dramatic event, a little explosion.

At every hand, the suburbs were sleeping.

I glanced at my watch—five minutes to go. I was on time. I'm always on time—what am I afraid of, that the world won't wait? In the night away to the north-west I heard a siren start up. Good, any cops in the area would be headed away from us. Nervously, my hand went to my inside pocket: no, not the old service revolver, just my passport and my police registration. My business card from work associating me with the higher cultural activities of the city—if the shit

hit I would be able, especially in those clothes, to insist I was someone and should be treated with due regard. Overhead now I became aware of a helicopter and was tempted to freeze. But it was high, high, and heading north-west. Pausing at the mouth of Erdmann-Graeser-Weg, I succumbed to a moment of anxious listening. But you must never look, never listen—just do it, that's the modern spirit. Don't feel anything. Don't be aware. Keep going straight ahead, looking neither from side to side nor down. Poverty, the homeless, vicious outbreaks, the purging of ethnic minorities, the ploughing under of the indigenous, the young, the old, the halt, the enthusiastic, the friendly—hesitation about any of this can only hinder you as you plunge towards whatever it is that you deserve. Well, I mustn't sound superior, this is precisely how I operate. But then when I did pause, there in the night street my actual heart was pounding so hard that it felt like a bell was tolling in my chest and all I could hear was the tumult of the protesting city.

In every direction the silence was profound.

I started up the little weg and in the night the old-fashioned lamps as I passed them gave off a gassy, green-tinged light that warmed the failing heart. And there, in the shadows at the near end of the bridge, was a large shape with a beard.

It was him, of course it was him, who else would it be, but for a moment in the long-shadowed night his face looked like Judgement Day, eyes in sockets deepened by the foolishness they've seen. And before their grim measure I now presented myself.

'Rumour,' he hissed, 'when are you going to get changed?'

'I am changed.'

His eye, running judgementally up and down my black best, suggested that I was once again foolishly wrong. His idea of right consisted of the big black leather coat, the black boots with their hidden cavity, black jeans and a death-metal tee—also an art-opening rig-out, but for a different artist. He glanced at his watch, then flicked an impatient hand to indicate that we should cross the bridge.

From below I could hear the water calling to me.

'Why are we going up here?' I whispered. (Why are we whispering? But we both were.)

He tapped his wristwatch.

I whispered, 'What about the dog?'

'I fixed the dog.'

I remembered him trying to fix it once before—had he brought the gun on this outing? 'How did you fix it?'

He put his finger to his mouth for hush and we tiptoed quietly past the dog bushes. No dog—good. But what had he done to achieve that? 'Are we going to tiptoe all the way?'

He turned on me. 'Rumour, I have this operation planned to the minute. Your job is to shut up and do what you're asked—for that you're getting a hundred thou. Try not to blow it.' And led us on. We emerged onto Argentinische Allee, where the traffic was still heavy. Side by side we plodded, grimly—Doc and Wyatt on the way to the OK Corral. My heart was like that bird trapped in the S-Bahn, it wanted to escape my chest. Our apartment block came up on the left. Glancing in I could see Bernadette in the big room, bent over something on the table. Maybe she was writing a new poem? I wanted to fly like an angel, to hover over her and watch the words come out. There was something so lovely about the picture she made and here I was, out in the night, looking in—it was as though, Sachsenhausen, Stevens, I had drawn the lot that said, You do the shit stuff, and I had a moment of poor, poor pitiful me.

She didn't lift her head.

Then we were past and ahead was the lamppost where the camera was attached. Helplessly, I glanced up—I imagined a bored cop in some grim basement room saying, 'The guilty ones always look at the camera.' I sent Stevens an inquiring glance and he gave a tight little nod. So he'd fixed it too. I had to say, his planning was impressive. Maybe this was going to work?

As we crossed the road and began up Sven-Hedin Strasse, he began. 'The embassy is eighty metres on the left, just around this curve. The guard is standing on the footpath— unless a car is arriving, he never goes out to the road, so he can't see any further this way than the bend of that hedge. Just before that there's a gateway, it's kind of set back.' I knew exactly where he meant, in the winter months there was an organic produce stall that set itself up in this gateway, away from the blast of the street. There were two tall wrought iron gates with, as I remembered it, uprights that ended in sharp points. 'We go quietly up there, through the gates, up the bank and across the lawn. You come behind me. Don't creep, Rumour. Walk upright, walk slowly, look relaxed. Okay, silence now.'

But there wasn't any silence to be had. For a start, the zapfen were like little bombs that exploded as we trod. Then there was my heart which was louder than a jackhammer— the 'guard' Stevens had mentioned was no guard. He was a uniformed German cop and carried a machine gun. Normally you didn't see this, the thing was slung on his back, but I had been up here with Fred, who had whispered to me about it—I knew that gun was there and that it was there for us. I could feel that gun and Stevens's gun calling to each other, they wanted to kiss, they wanted to get hot together. With me in the middle. I knew from movies how after the firing you looked down at the sudden holes in your chest, where the blood was now spurting—you looked surprised, and right on the point of realising something, when your mouth went slack . . . Also, there was the comedy aspect—I was right behind Stevens now and when he slowed I was, as in ten thousand bumbling-crimo flicks, in danger of bumping into him. Thus as we progressed I was constantly on the edge of releasing, like a flight of birds, a soprano burst of laughter.

What stoppered that was a kind of amazement at Stevens. True, he still looked like a minor bandito from *The Good, The Bad and The Ugly*, but when we came to the gate, which looked impregnable, with a large lock hanging on a heavy chain, he pointed to the hinges on the right-hand end. The gate had been lifted so that the pins—I have heard these called pindles—had come clear of the round-hole bit. Unable to contain himself, Stevens turned his back to the gate and mimed how he had lifted it, presumably earlier in the day. He caught my eye, asked for my admiration. I gave it unstintingly—thumbs up to you, Stevens.

I wished Bernadette could see this. Bernadette, it's all working. He's a genius. We're going to be rich!

From his pocket he produced a pair of black leather gloves and stuffed his fat fingers into them, peeling back the cuff on one side so that his fancy watch was exposed. Now he tilted it to the light—clearly we were on some kind of schedule—then took hold of the gate and eased it open. He wiggled two gloved fingers at me, miming us walking, then slipped through. We went, as he'd said, up a little bank.

Now we were on private property.

Along the fenceline there was a parallel line of boundary trees, dark, slim and upright, and against them we moved in the prescribed manner, slowly, looking relaxed—don't mind us, we're just burglars—towards the embassy. Away across the grass to our left, the large house stood white in the night air. There were lighted windows, and a door which was open onto a first-floor balcony, but no one was out on it. I kept one eye on that, that worried me. But I was letting Stevens do the thinking.

Here was the embassy boundary. It was marked by a border garden, which we trod through, leaving, I thought, good footprints—I would have to throw these shoes away. Or, no, they were a bit expensive for that, I would just hide them. I would of course scrub the mud off them first, with some scrubbing device which I would itself scrub, and then I would wipe both shoes and scrubbing device free of fingerprints. Yes, that should cover it.

Beyond the garden was a little downslope and then the fence. This looked tricky, the fence was high and had three strands of barb running along the top. It was hurricane netting—old, rusty, but hurricane netting all the same (because it could stand in a hurricane? Must look that up). Stevens took us right close to the foot of it, where we squatted. Now I could see that immediately beyond it there was a drop of maybe two metres, then a narrow back-of-house pathway of concrete, then one of the embassy out-buildings. I saw now that this could be the building in the map that Stevens had showed me, it maybe had the same configuration. Fantastic, Stevens! But, an actual building, an official one at that— when confronted by it, it looked so solid. How could we ever get inside a thing like that? But my job was to do as I was told.

Stevens had his wrist out, was again angling the watch to the light. We waited. The guard-cop was maybe forty metres away, around the corner of the building nearest the street. My mind's eye found him and all I could think of was the weight of that gun, hanging on his shoulder for so many nights—you would be just itching to swing it down. I listened for his feet.

What a job, standing outside a gate for hours at a stretch, hell on the feet. Then I noticed that Stevens was listening too. One eye on his watch. In his fist now was a pair of pliers. I knew these pliers, red plastic sheathing on the handles—he'd taken them from my tool kit! They would incriminate me! Sure, they would snip the wire—but the snip would be loud! I opened my mouth to protest but Stevens immediately silenced me with an upright finger. He was listening closely now, intently.

Along Sven-Hedin Strasse footsteps could be heard—positively crunching the zapfen. Someone walking slowly. Stepping. That faint tack, tack—she was wearing heels.

Stevens's face was so completely intent. His pliers went to a wire near the bottom—not the actual bottom runner-wire, but the next one up—and stayed there. But his intent was on the footsteps, which stopped. There were voices—and immediately he snipped. The sound was loud, this was a snip heard around the world, and he followed it with another. The voices didn't continue, but there was what sounded like a shuffling of feet, small noises. My guess was, she'd asked the cop for a light. Then the footsteps started up again. Then stopped. Then started. Meantime the hole had become a metre tall and Stevens peeled back its edges and slipped through. He seemed almost agile and I was simply amazed, thrilled even, by my old friend. Obviously the heels were his doing, he'd found some woman, a prostitute I guessed, though I had never seen one in Zehlendorf, and paid her to be here, hence all the watch-checking, and now he was through the fence, had dropped to the path, and was beckoning me on.

Through I went. The path was concrete, old, pitted, with islands of moss. On tiptoes we went, away from the road, up the side of the building. There was a porch cut into the wall, with a door, it was the kind of place you might sleep the

124

night if you were homeless, and we stepped into it and were invisible. We gave each other the thumbs-up.

Stevens produced a tiny torch and showed me how to encircle it with my hand so that its light was hidden. This I shone on the keyhole while, on his knees, he began to try one after another from a mass of keys he had drawn from an inner pocket. They hung like a bunch of grapes but were all of the same type, with a long shaft and various tine-patterns at the end. How had he known to bring that particular type? Suddenly I was sure that he had crept along here at night, with binoculars, with a narrow torch beam, and, through the wire, made an assessment of the lock. Was this right? I had no idea and knew he would never tell me, but it was something like that—his assurance was so great.

It was strange standing there holding the torch, it took me back to hours spent with Dad, under the bonnet of the car, helping. A kind of mania comes over you, to hold the torch brilliantly—to be super-valuable by thinking ahead and guessing which tool he would want next and having it ready for him. Of course this always made the torch wobble but he was very patient. Afterwards he invariably said, 'You were very helpful, Martin,' and my little heart would swell.

Click.

Now Stevens, on his knees, looked up at me in grinning satisfaction. He turned the key, then beckoned my ear down to his mouth. 'The next bit is tricky,' he whispered. 'When I push the door, be ready to run—I don't know if there's an alarm. I didn't see one. But no one knows we're here, so they won't come round here first. Run back on your tiptoes, hoist me up the bank, then I'll pull you up. Don't wait—go along the trees, through the gate and stop there—got it?'

He turned the handle and pushed the door. It swung away from us into the interior darkness. There was a very loud ringing, the drilling sound of an angry bell, but that was only inside my head. No alarm.

'I didn't think so,' he whispered. 'I did a recce, didn't see a problem, but you have to plan for everything.' In he went, and I followed.

Now my brain had a little seizure. We were in the building on his map and suddenly I badly wanted to remember what the room number had been. 323B? B332? I felt I should have retained this. I felt like a passenger.

We were in a corridor, dark, with doors down either side. The air smelled musty, old, as though it had been shut in. Ahead, at the end, there was a door with glass panels through which a bare courtyard could be seen, with nightlights playing on it. The floor beneath us was dull, standard-issue office linoleum. Our feet squeaked.

Along to our left there were three doors—if my memory of the plan was to be trusted, we should attack the middle one. At head height on the doors there were numbers in peeling red plastic. Stevens's gloved torch shone: 411. 'This is it,' he whispered.

'The number didn't have a 4 in it.'

'Must've been changed,' he said firmly and took hold of the handle. These door openings! Each time my teeth were gritted against the howl of an alarm. It was all I could do not to squeeze my eyes shut tight.

Chapter Nine

If I got a hundred thousand now, this was the question: what would I do? Yes, okay, escape Sachsenhausen, that's obvious. Get Bernadette out of here. Go home to New Zealand with enough money to declare the trip a fabulous sojourn that happened to have an attractive fiscal element—it's always cool to behave as though money effortlessly attaches itself to you.

Probably I could get a suit job in the culture machinery, one of those things where you have to attend four openings a week—culture is always telling itself that what's needed are more project managers.

I used to want to run a bookshop. But there are lots of bookshops.

Another little dream was to open a movie house. Say on Waiheke—there's a beautiful old disused cinema there. Run an art programme, bring in all the greats that I've only ever read about. Live at the movies.

But Waiheke Island has been turning into Monaco, a helipad for taste-free cash. Everything interesting is on the way out, I'm maybe fifteen years too late. Plus, even art movies are in the end somehow an escape.

So lately the focus has shifted. There's still an emphasis on bringing art to the people but there has to be a quixotic element. Somehow an Everest, an impossibility. Dealer gallery—no, think of who you'd have to toady to. Then, on a random wind, a new idea blew into town. Beneath a blue sky it flapped its white pages, opening them so that words could tumble like rain down onto the parched hordes below:

Poetry. That was the thing. I could make a poetry bookshop. Nothing but—see the purity of that? A business that the entire world declares there's no money in: to make a go of it. I can already see myself, wry on the front of *NZ Business*. Bernadette as Special Adviser (and secretly scribbling lines on the back of invoices). Starving. That's it. To visibly, publicly starve for art—this really appealed.

It would have to be in Wellington, of course—where poetry lives. And I would not be a follower of the scene but a player. Dedicated. Knowledgeable. Declared by all to be officially a good thing.

It would be important to find exactly the right name for the shop. Something . . . evocative. *The Sphinx*—no, too inscrutable. But I should start thinking a lot about that.

So there, in the corridor of the Nigerian embassy building in suburban Berlin, I was thinking of poetry. I thought, I am doing this crime for poetry.

Stevens pushed at 411. The door started to swing, then, as though it had seen all the B-movies, its hinges began to creak. Louder and louder, like monstrous jaws opening. Then it bumped into something and, with a little shudder, stopped. A trickle of sweat ran down my neck—noble sweat, was what I thought. I thought, I am really earning it tonight.

Beyond the door lay darkness, a spooky dark, and Stevens paused to assess the situation. He could order me in and, if there was a monster then I would be the one to get eaten, which was only fair as he had done all the heavy lifting so far. But if there was no monster then he should go, so as to retain the initiative. The glory. He risked his torch. In that charged darkness, the light inside his hand was magic, supernatural. Its muffled beam went in through the crack to expose the exact nature of our chamber of wonders.

Cardboard boxes.

The room was packed high with them, stacked irregularly, solid cubes waiting to be muscled into place by the builders of the pyramids. One had fallen to block the door—when Stevens kicked it it gave a dead thud, as though it was stuffed with papers. We shouldered our way in. Yes—the room was a file-office, a dead-letter storeroom. Dust floated in his fistful of light. 'Shut the door,' he said. But I didn't want to, I didn't want to be shut in here with the dead air, it was already hard enough to breathe.

But, okay, any barrier between us and the cop's gun was a good thing and I did as I was told. And now Stevens's torch began to search. There was no order here, the boxes had just been dumped, maybe after a shift of offices?—stacked so the maximum number might be got into the room. However, there were a couple of gaps, tall like vertical crevasses, and a particularly promising one opened at two o'clock from us— after checking in every other direction, Stevens tried to go through it. But he was too fat.

We could have repacked the room but that looked like a job for Rubik. Eventually Stevens gave the order. 'Okay, Random, do your stuff.'

The old-cardboard smell is not my favourite and right now it was a mile up my nose. Handing him my jacket, I edged into the gap. I felt like a speleologist going through a cave opening, an iceman going inside a wall of white. Except that it was anything but cold—there was a slight clammy warmth about the boxes that made me reluctant to touch them. When most of my body was encased I stretched an arm back for the torch.

'What?' said Stevens.

'Give it.'

'No, no, I have to direct operations. Press ahead, more to the left. Hurry, Random, the longer we're here the greater the chance that something unplanned will occur.' So, alone, unlit, I felt my way forward through the solid volume of the room. There was a faint glow on the ceiling that told me where Stevens was and I forced myself to edge away from it. It was clear that I was on some kind of path, very narrow, that had been left on purpose. It zigged and zagged, in some places I had to use my weight and squeeze. A tower of boxes would ease away a little—what if they fell? Damp cardboard pressed my cheeks, gripped my thighs. Then, down in a corner, I heard a rustle.

'Stevens,' I hissed. 'There's something here.'

'What? Describe.'

'There's something moving. Down in the corner.'

'Random! It's a rat! Come on, jesus, it's just some little thing—it's probably a fucking earwig. Get on with it!'

But you know how things get bigger in the dark. I was not in any situation where I could run. I didn't want to face, alone, in the dark, the Giant Nigerian Archive Earwig (GNAE), with pincers of steel and a sting which would leave me, paralysed but living, suspended there between the boxes as a food source for its young. I kicked out, hard, intending to make a big-animal noise—and my foot hurt. 'Ow,' I said.

'What now?'

'My foot hit something.'

'Like a desk?'

'Yeah, could be.'

'Good boy,' said Stevens. 'Okay, get round the back of it. Hurry, Random.' But now the Gnae stirred again, I heard it clearly, it rustled, it scuttled. This was down towards my ankles—I was unable to bend and as I thought about this I realised that my trouser leg had ridden up and that square inches of my shin were exposed. I hated that! The Gnae was,

130

I knew, completely aware of this sector of naked, defenceless skin. Down there, the hairs twitched. I remembered this sensation from skin-diving—I always wanted the rubber suit to cover every inch.

But I was born a hero. I went 'Hahhh,' low, a sheep-harrying sound, and kicked out again. God, it was dark. But when I moved forward the hard outline of the desk pressed against my thigh. I made my way round it, hah-ing as I went. 'I'm at the back of the desk,' I shouted. At the same time I stamped my feet, fiercely.

'Quiet, Random, for christ sakes. Now, left hand side as you face it, second-to-top drawer—and speed it up.'

I could feel that an opening had been made behind the desk, as though someone liked to come here and sit—a hidey-hole. There were boxes on top of it, though. My fingers explored—yes, here was the first drawer. And, yes, below it the second. There was a little dangling hoop of metal, a drawer-pull—in my mind it glowed dully, worn by the fingers of time. I pulled on it and, slowly, the drawer came sliding out.

'I'm opening it,' I called loudly, stamping and kicking.

'Shut up, Rumour! Okay, now, put your hand in.'

But the Gnae had gone very quiet and I didn't want to put my hand in.

'What's happening, Random?' hissed Stevens.

Have you ever heard about those people who go around putting rat traps inside your letterbox? Or rattlesnakes? Okay now, forcing myself: here I go. I look down at my hand—the left one, which I use less—and even in this near-total darkness I can just make out the pale boniness of it. Its spectral shine—Christ's hand shone like this just before the nail went through. My right comes over and grabs the left by the wrist and forces it, as though it's an implement, to feel inside the drawer. Goodbye, old friend, I loved you well—and

131

my fingers crawl over the wooden bottom. Slightly splintery, powdery with dust. Nothing to feel. Nothing.

'Random, jesus!'

'There's nothing here.'

'Yes, there is! Go deeper!'

The pain you have been bracing yourself for and then there's nothing, it's as emptying as a blood-letting. I sink to my knees, begin to thrust my arm determinedly. The drawer goes back the full length of the desk, my arm is in nearly to the shoulder. Now I am reminded of my Uncle Murray, in the late-morning cowshed, his arm shoulder-deep up the backside of a poor cow whose calf had arrived in parts and were they all out? Boldly, my fingers tickle the corners. Nothing. 'Still nothing,' I call.

'I'm coming,' he growls, and I hear him begin to heft boxes. There's a dull thud and I know, soon the cop will come, or else the dawn. It's all over—it's all nothing.

'Hang on,' I say.

'What is it?'

'Hang on.'

'What? What?'

'Right at the back—there's . . . hang . . . on. Yeah, listen, right at the very, very back, there's something pinned to the end wall of the drawer. Feels like a bit of cardboard, I can't . . .'

'Don't tear it! Wait! Random!'

'There's a bit of cardboard with what feels like a drawing pin stuck in it and then, are you listening?'

'Fuck you.'

'And then at the top there is, wait for it—the crowd will tell you—wait . . . Okay: at the top is a piece of string which goes through a little hole in the top of the card.'

Now the Gnae rustled again. But it was, I could hear

132

clearly now, away in the corner of the room, and suddenly I was no longer afraid. I'd found it! Nothing could touch me! Bernadette! Everyone! Look, look, my fingers are following the string, it's frail but I am sensitive, I'm getting one finger under it, I'm pulling it up and back over the end wall of the drawer: there was, in the silence, a small 'clonk'.

'Random?'

'I think it's a key.'

For once Stevens didn't speak. Was he praying? Was he giving thanks? I was. My fingernail worked on the drawing pin. Bloody hurt, but I kept at it. It eased out enough for me to get finger and thumb to pinch its top and twist. And you know how it is with reluctant drawing pins, once you get to this stage you know it's only a matter of time.

I gathered the metal piece—surely a key?—and gently drew it, with the card, now unpinned, on the end of the twist of string, towards me. I lifted it clear and enclosed it tightly in my fist in case the Gnae made a last and desperate assault. I said, 'It is a key.'

'Good!' There was an audible release of breath. 'Okay, good—let's get the fuck out of here!'

We were noisier than we might have been getting back up the wall, but it didn't seem to matter. Quickly—walk, don't run—we crossed the garden, went along the line of trees, through the gate which, behind us, Stevens lifted back into place. Then we began to tiptoe away down Sven-Hedin Strasse. It was amazing to think that all that was between us and the black hole at the end of the cop's tommy-gun was the slight curve of the road, but it seemed to be enough. It was working. We were getting away with it.

The key was, of course, now in Stevens's pocket.

We returned to the fountain. I thought that this was a risk but Stevens pointed out that we didn't have pocketfuls of dosh nor had a siren gone off so why not? And it was brilliant to be there, nice—it was only ten-thirty, the pizza place was still pitching 'em up, and out in the middle of the circle of dark grass the fountain was playing our song. We sat side by side on the bench like pensioners, it was a happy-sunset moment, the end of a movie, when you look back and are gratefully aware of all the connected decisions which got you to here. Stevens produced the key and fondled it briefly before handing it over. It was nickel-plated, about the size you might use on a small padlock. Shapely—a quality key, which pleased the hand upon which it lay—though, was this really the key to a safe deposit box? I thought that might look more . . . precious. Its little label was a square of card, hand-cut, like a postage stamp (remember them?). There was a small hole where the drawing pin had gone through, if you held it up, through this hole you could see your future: golden light and a sense of there being no speed limit on the highway. I was profoundly grateful. Then Stevens snatched it back. While I had been looking through it he'd seen something. 'See?' he breathed.

I peered down. There on the card—off the end of his black-rimmed, cracked thumbnail were inky lines, pale. 'It's an en,' he said. This didn't mean a lot (I know—printer's measure, from Scrabble—yeah, yeah) and I frowned, but he was in such a cheered-up frame that he didn't growl. Instead he explained nicely. 'For Nigeria.' And we looked at each other.

You know, your heart really does soar. Mine was going up like a freed balloon, as I watched the fountain rise into the night I was filled by lightness and awe. A hundred thousand euro. Actually, it's not a king's ransom and I knew that. It takes more than a year's salary to change your life. But to get it for nothing, it was like for once getting something you actually wanted for Christmas.

Suddenly the biggest thing was, Stevens. He continued to have a pong that walked like an Egyptian. His beard continued to be the Edward Lear Memorial Home For Nesting Birds, plus his fingernails meant I could never take him home to meet my mum. But all of this had become irrelevant—it was just part of his being a fabulous character, an original.

And—the ultimate accolade—a good guy.

A young woman came across from the S-Bahn station and, tracked by Stevens's eyes, made her hurried way on into the night. 'Stevens,' I said, 'she's just a kid—man, she's about Sally's age.'

'Old enough to bleed,' he growled, 'old enough to slaughter.'

I had heard this charming phrase before, it went together with early-opening pubs and brown-eyeing the bride's mother. Stevens, perhaps now sensing a gap opening in the bond between us, said quickly, 'A hundred thousand isn't actually all that much, you know, Random.' This was in the nicely-explaining voice. 'You've got three kids. You're, what, fifty-something?—any retirement income?' Well, he knew the answer to that one. 'Okay, so you've earned your share, no question. But maybe you'd like to be in for a bigger slice?'

'How d'you mean?'

'Well, you know: I put up my house. So far I spent I guess twenty thou. I've got a trip to the blacklands coming up, that won't cost diddly—a bit of bribery, some expensive cocktails with Mr Abraham Ido . . . air-tickets, hotels, women—you have to be seen with someone there, and not just some bar-girl neither.'

135

'Hey, that was amazing,' I said, 'you getting that girl to distract the cop.'

'A masterstroke,' he said, 'like you don't realise. I was doing a bit of a scout one day, I saw his eyes follow a skirt and I just knew.' He nodded, cool as. However, there was a faint pinkness came over him and I saw that he'd also had some kind of an entanglement with this woman—maybe paid for some fun. Which figured. Though he talked like the king of the stickmen, Stevens never in my experience had had a girlfriend. Never get involved, he always said, never give anyone an intimate angle on you. A German prostitute, there was something about that that I found quite . . . stirring . . .

'So,' he said gently, 'if you wanted to kick in, say, thirty thou, your share would be five.'

'Euro?' And he could hear the faint horror in my voice.

'It's up to you. Euro in, euro out. Or dollars Enzed, if you like. Random, I don't need the money, I could fund this no probs on my own.'

I was torn and I took the easy way out. 'I'd have to talk to Bernadette,' I said.

'Of course.' But his face closed and as it did I saw my poetry bookshop quietly slipping below the waves.

As we sauntered homeward through the night, there was no further need to converse. We'd done so well and could in all conscience have headed for a bar.

But I had other ideas. The truth was, I wanted to get away from Stevens. I wanted to sit by myself and feel humble. That I would be able to stand before Bernadette, before my kids, and say, I brought home the bacon. I could see a kind of ceremony where, while I was watching TV sport, Bernadette carried in a tray with my dinner. The kids would be casually strewn about the room—looking up, I would realise they'd been waiting. Beside the plate a beaded glass with just that perfect quarter-inch of head, and as I looked down into it for that first delicious sip I would notice (I guess the foam sort of parts like the Red Sea) something stuck to the bottom. Down through the beer I would read, in Bernadette's disciplined hand, these words: Martin Rumsfield—A Good Provider. And they would all come and hang off my neck.

Actually, there was a specific item I wanted to get Fred. No, not get—to do. I was going to teach him to read. Funny, I always thought that when my ship came in I would buy things for everyone. Now that it had, I understood: now I was going to have the satisfaction, the patience, to actually *do* things with them. I would spend hours with Fred while he sounded words out. For the rest of his life he would say, My dad taught me to read. And Sandy—I would teach Sandy to talk.

For Bernadette? For Bernadette I will, as has been noted, spend more time with the kids—so get off my back. But it is when I think of giving her what she really wants that I start to get excited. We are going to have another baby! Personally, I am against this, the thought fills me with exhaustion, but, as I remind myself, now we will be able to afford a nanny or somesuch, a cleaner-up, someone to do the baby-holding. And now, with my new patience, I will be much better about crying in the night. A new baby: that will bring us at least three years of complete happiness. The thought has me skipping.

And for myself? I think we all know the answer to that. CD retailers of Berlin, please stand by your shelves.

*

137

At the back steps of our house I shook hands with Stevens and watched as he made his clumsy way in through the downstairs window. He was supposed to have been banished, but, I asked myself: how will Bernadette feel now?

She was in the computer room and when I came in she gave me a particular look that I had come to beware: gimlet-eyed. They say this about gunfighters. A gimlet is a kind of narrow pointy thing for making a hole, my dad used to have one in his shed—I guess it means a look hard enough to make a hole in you. She was at the keyboard and looked up at me with the light of the screen on one side of her face. I wanted to speak with her, to tell her that now everything was different. But as you get older you get wiser.

The gimlets shifted slowly to the screen and there I saw, at the head of some file she had Googled up, the words *The Nigeria Scam—A Short History*. 'I thought we might be aided by a bit of research,' she said.

There was no triumph in this, only disgust. Not with me. Or, not only with me. With the world, with herself. 'Read it,' she said.

'What does it say, darling?' I thought the darling was good, here. I refused to feel daunted.

'It says that your Mr what was it?'

'Preed? Goodson?'

'Yes, and the other one.'

I struggled to remember the names Stevens had given me. 'Yeah, there's another guy—um, yeah: Mr Barry Kelly.'

'Mr Kelly,' said Bernadette. 'And they are the ones who had all this money—Martin, just look at this.' But I wasn't going near the computer. When she saw this she said, 'He probably did get an email—was it an email?'

She was talking about Stevens, whose name could not be spoken. I have to say that I was, after recent events, offended on his behalf. It was kind of nice, this, the way I knew that I could ride out her storm and then give her the good news that would adjust the tilt of her chin. Calmly, I nodded.

'He probably did,' she said. 'But so did thousands of people. Millions. You haven't understood this thing. It isn't *one* person, scamming over and over. It's the same scam, worked by queues of Nigerians. Look at the names here: Mrs Eunice Kamsi, except that she spells it 'Enuice', whose father was Chairman of the ELEME Special Oil Trust Fund—Chief Ugochukwu Kamsi. Reverend Mr Ngomo Bird, whose father was Chief Bird. Look,' she was scrolling, then reading, 'Mr Denis Ntumba, whose uncle was Big Chief Ntumba—Denis wants your help to retrieve his uncle's gold and diamonds worth one hundred and seventy-five million of which he will give you fifteen percent. Or, look, Mr Chappie Igo, who wants—ah, Martin . . .'

'Finished?'

Now she gave me the special reserve look that kills off those who try to jump the queue at the super or nip into her parking place. I dug in. 'So you don't want to know how the mission went?'

'Mission?'

'It was, actually. He'd done a recce, he had the right gear, everything timed—and it went like clockwork. Listen, he'd even hired a professional chick to distract the gate cop, because he'd observed that the guy liked a short skirt.'

'So and?'

This expression was a fuck-you favourite of Sally's and to hear Bernadette using it, in this moment, frankly, I was well pissed off. 'So and go to bed,' I said, 'and cry yourself to sleep because we're stuck in our lives until you write a poem worth a hundred thou or stick it up your nose.' And I poked my tongue at her, which made her allow a tiny smile.

But also in her face was a slight incredulity, that I would mention her poetry, which was a totally off-limits subject, and mention it in such a cavalier fashion. I saw the thought occur: maybe I did have something to tell? Immediately I said, as resentfully as possible, 'I'm going to bed.'

Chapter Ten

Ah, bed. The crystal ship, the island of dreams. The place where despair lies down and has a smoke. I've often wished I was a smoker and I'm sure it could be very easily done, but I'm so oral, I just know I'd have one in my hand and one in my mouth at every breathing moment—here, in the dark, it might be nice to draw a flame through the air. These days we are in the front bedroom, the smaller one, so that Fred can enjoy spreading his toys over a bigger landscape. With the window open you get a lot of traffic noise from Argentinische Allee, I lay and listened to the tyres and surrendered to the sensation that I was being carried away, on a magic carpet, ankle-deep in banknotes.

Eventually, from her side of the great divide—Sandy was lying between us—Bernadette whispered, 'So it went okay?'

'Who wants to know?'

'I'm trying to humour you.'

'No need, I'm a humour-free zone, we know that.'

This went on for some time, I won't bore you. But in fact I was struggling to hold back, and finally her interest seemed sufficiently genuine.

I told it my way, with lots of minor embellishments—I said that the house with a balcony had a guy who kept coming out for a cigarette, that the cop was so close I could hear what the girl said to him—and I managed to keep a kind of flatness in my voice which conveyed to her that I really was excited. And she sat up in the dark and looked down at me. I had my arms up behind my head, lying there I probably looked like Belmondo in *À Bout de Souffle*. Probably. 'So where is this key now?'

'In his pocket.'

'Which is where you are.'

But this was not said unkindly and, after a particularly noisy truck had been allowed to pass, she said into the following silence, 'So you really think there might actually be something in this?'

I was on the point of telling her about the poetry bookshop when I decided that restraint was the right note. Then I remembered that for the real jackpot we were going to have to invest some of our savings and that was definitely not a conversation I presently wanted to start upon. So I simply said, 'Yep.'

'Really . . .' And finally I heard some excitement. I decided to let this moment stretch out. Yes, I felt good. I was with the most feet-on-the-ground person I knew and my dream was still on its legs. Then I had a further thought and I was just on the point of mentioning that we would now be able to have another baby when she said, 'So tell me again about this girl.'

'Darling, listen.'

'No, tell me, Martin. There was a cop and the cop needed distracting and he found a girl.'

'Yeah, and it worked like clockwork. See, we had to have—'

'He doesn't even speak German.'

'So and?'

'So which prostitutes are well-educated enough to speak English?'

'Oh, all kinds . . . You know, for the international trade . . .'

'He didn't get any international trade prostitute,' she said firmly. She was still sitting up. I could just make out her face and while I watched a frown began to form on it. Then she got out of bed.

She's always been like this, always been the one who makes a cup of tea in the night, who when you stumble out for a pee at 3am you find with a novel beneath a low light; as soon as you speak she switches it off and heads back to bed. Me, if I can't sleep I stay put, I like to drift. Now as I lay there I was thinking that when she came back I would say what I had decided, about a new baby—even a hundred thou should see us right for that. I mean, a million wouldn't be enough but why shouldn't she have what she wants, since I was going to? Babies are always a bit of a gamble, all of ours came out of the blue, you can't plan that. But one more wouldn't be wrong, and I could imagine three months of intense sex, that special baby-making fucking that is the best kind.

As I entertained this notion I felt wonderfully, expansively generous. Bringing new life into the world, that is always something to be proud of.

Bernadette came back and shook my leg, hard—harshly even. 'Sally's not in her bed.'

Part One ends

Chapter Eleven

Sometimes I think about what might have come into my head that time in the Wairarapa when, aged nine, I was in the river and starting to drown. It's a moment both so repressed and so frequently remembered that it's hard now to tell what really happened and what has accreted over the years during successive retellings. The one thing I am sure of is the surface, which, seen from its underside, was what my eyes were fixed on—the flexing ceiling of the room I was in, something that had always been looked down upon now seen as that which you had to climb towards. The shock of that perspective—its simple freshness. But that I think is what I focused on, later. On what I could see. On what I could handle—I always remember the profusion of bubbles as my arms flapped. Is it true that at that moment I started to understand the threat of violent change that lies below the surface of the world? That as I struggled upwards, mouth-first, to snatch a breath, I was understanding that the everyday which you rely on can collapse beneath you without warning? The ground you step on, the river you walk beside—the way that any of these familiar and friendly things can change and become a mortal threat.

The window of her bedroom was open. A large, white-framed oblong of glass, it swung on its strong German hinges into her room like a wing, leaving a dark hole in through which the night flowed. I climbed onto the sill, dropped to the grass.

I was wearing a pair of the brightly-patterned boxer shorts

that Bernadette had bought for me to sleep in and to be out in them gave the feeling of having had to run outside because of a fire. I shivered below the window: where would a teenager go? But it wasn't cold. The late summer night air was warm and inviting, full of possibilities. At a jog, I went barefoot, down the concrete path, which glowed white before me. To either side were bushes, dark, like places where unseen things might happen. Lights in windows, low buildings, trees. Nothing moving.

Darkness. Where the buildings ended, a grassy downslope to the lake. Lake-edge, bench, jetty, all empty. I went out onto the jetty and looked down into the shallows. Nothing. It was such a warm, pleasant night to be out. Even the water looked inviting. This was false, I knew that.

I searched the ground near the bench for anything, any clue. In the lakeside bushes I looked for underwear left lying—you see that, on the ground outside the U-Bahn stations in the morning, underwear abandoned—what does it mean? Somehow pressed flat, as though its sense of purpose has leaked away. Or shoes, sneakers, just left. That life that teenagers have, at bus-stops or around a bench-seat. Kids without enough money to be anywhere but who won't go home; hair slicked back, in cheap fashion clobber, cigarettes held like experiments. Empty beer cans, crushed, in a semi-circle.

Standing again on the jetty I addressed the night. I said her name, low, urgent: 'Sally!'

The word choked a little as it came out. Walking the lake-edge, which was making small invitational mouth-sounds, I made myself say it again, 'Sally, Sally,' but these were words addressed to bushes, to the downslope of grass. I kept saying this word, hopelessly, doing my duty, all the way back up the path to the house.

Bernadette was standing on the steps of the patio, arms folded. In her crushed old white nightie she looked terrible—pale, puffed-up, angry-worried. As I came up she said, flat with anger: 'She was the prostitute.' Her head inclined fractionally down towards the keller window where Stevens was. The window was dimly lit and I could smell cigarette smoke rising from it.

'Did he say so?'

She nodded, too angry to speak.

'You asked him?'

This didn't merit an answer. 'What did he say?' I was wondering how it had been done—did she stand outside the window and shout down? But I hadn't heard anything. No, she kneeled and put her head in—now I saw that her nightdress had two dark spots at the knees.

'She wore those clothes.'

'Right,' I said, 'and so she spoke to the cop—then what?'

Bernadette produced a look that withered every ounce of hope in me. She was utterly grim and I felt something rising inside, an insistence that she was getting carried away, that this wasn't necessarily so bad. Teenagers, cigarettes, the benches outside the U-Bahn, these images rose as evidence of a world going about its business, but I didn't air them. Instead I asked, 'What did he say happened next? He had it all planned. It was all planned, Bernadette!'

Disgust and anger were choking her. I saw that I was rendered permanently loathsome in her eyes and I became angry myself: nothing had happened, yet. This was all a big, blown-up drama. At any minute Sal was going to stroll up, full of the night air—sure, in her slut clothes, but it wasn't a hanging offence—and say she'd met some kids for a drink.

'He said,' said Bernadette, 'that she was to walk around the block and come back here,' now her head indicated

Sally's window, 'where there'd be one hundred euro waiting for her.'

'And was there?'

Every time her eyes made contact with mine, I was made smaller. 'What?' she spat out, incredulous.

'Was the money there? Is it there? Did she come home and get it?'

'I didn't ask.' And at this she turned and went inside, leaving the impression of a burning white shape hanging in the air.

I stood, swaying a little, trying to think. I didn't want to speak with Stevens. But I knew I had to.

*

Down in the keller with Stevens, this is my idea of down. This is being in an anteroom of Hell. He was sitting deep in the oxblood couch, an arm out to either side along its back, a swimmer resting after thirty lengths. I stood on the carpet before him. There were various sitting options but there I stood. I guess my bottom lip was out. Stevens wouldn't meet my eye. There used to be a song on a CD by Little Village that said, 'Don't bug me when I'm working,' and Stevens was playing this song. His clouded face said that a difficult equation was close to being solved.

The keller was tight around me, as though I was in a fist. He had filled it with crap, boxes from which stuff tumbled, filthy clothes, a dead TV. All of this pressed in upon me. I stood on his carpet, lip out, swaying, and waited. Finally his heavy gaze drifted towards mine and I said, 'We're going to the police.'

'No police.'

His jaw was set, this made his beard jut, and around his eyes sweat was forming, so that the skin there looked as though it was crawling off to escape him. We looked frankly into each other. How could I ever have thought this disgusting thing was a good guy? I needed incarceration. But I was choking on a huge lump of worry. Forcing the words out I said, 'Any idea where she might be?'

'Random—Random, man,' he said, 'she's just a little twat, they all have to bleed some time. Let her have her fun.'

The phrase he'd used, *old enough to slaughter,* came into my head, I felt sick with self-disgust and I had to get out of there. I began to drag myself up the ladder. 'A hundred thousand,' said Stevens but I kept climbing. 'Random, listen, she'll come back. Jesus, give it time.' I was at the top now, starting to clamber out the window. I felt both heavy and shapeless, as though I was made of porridge. At the same time anxiety was giving me terrible surges of energy. 'Random, if you bring in the cops now you're out.' I felt as though Stevens had my legs, was pulling me down—I could see the surface and just had to keep fighting up for a breath. 'That's what they're for,' he said grimly, 'get over it.' I was gasping when, finally, I stepped out into the night. I had let my daughter enter his thoughts. And now she was gone.

The poetry bookshop shrank inside me to the size of a pinhead and then vanished.

How could I be thinking about that, now? But it happened.

From the lake, a bird called, a desperate sound. In my lungs the night air burned. I shook myself, tried to find the way forward. Not so easy. I rocked a little. It was as though, in letting Sal be taken, I had lost the thing in me that made me go.

What it takes to learn.

Then I saw that along to my left there was a window open. It was Sally's window, and from it I could hear Bernadette's voice. She was on the phone. As I listened, I realised she was talking to Sal. I ran inside. Oh, the relief! Oh, the feeling of Sal coming back to life! I burst into the computer room. Bernadette was putting the phone down. Her face had been soft and sweet from talking to Sal—as I watched, that drained away and a raw anger returned. I recoiled. 'But you found her,' I said.

'Just her mailbox.'

'Ah . . .' But Bernadette had been clever, to think of Sally's mobile—her handy, as the Germans call them. Sal's was so small, like a little organ, an ear, a tongue, curved slightly so that it could nest inside your hand, but so full, so loaded— these little phones, with which the kids can run the world. Now I stared into Bernadette's eyes. In there I could also see myself: stupid, criminally thick. No, worse: I was as repulsive as Stevens—I was one with him. No, even *worse*, because I was supposed to have been better. I stared into all that—and felt a resistance forming. It was kind of like a frown. I was having a thought. That sounds insane, or as though I had been drugged down. But it was the feeling: I'm having a thought. What was it? Yes, as I stared into Bernadette's terrible face there was something I knew I should be thinking.

Her face is like a lake, it has so many moods. It has something white about it, that's the Irish in her, there's even a green that can be caught when the wind is from the North. Her blood comes quickly, and drains; as the changes come over her her face speaks them. She has always been for me the face of judgement—maybe it's because she's a believer? Whereas I am the great jelly of the crossroads. I have always ceded moral authority to her and, down in my bones, accepted her pronouncements.

Bernadette's face now giving me the final judgement.

And yet.

I have made a religion of escape. My entire life has consisted of me offering the world my single talent, which is for finding a way out. Faced by the rampant headmaster, I produce a plausible lie and get us all off. That is why they want me at Sachsenhausen, why I am here in Germany: because when I am faced with the intractable consequences, I wriggle and squirm, and—

'Yeah, but that bloody handy . . .' I said to Bernadette. There now in the computer room, speaking in the industrial glow from the screen; we're two feet apart and facing each other, and maybe I've found something. 'Remember?' It's coming to me: the wriggle room. 'Remember, what she told us—remember how she talked us into buying it.' Bernadette trying to remember—see, she doesn't want to hate me. Us staring into each other's eyes, digging this out. *You'll always know where I am*, she said—remember? There's a website.'

'What?'

'Didn't she tell us: *You'll always be able to know where I am because there's a website for if you lose your phone.*'

'So?'

'So there's a website for if you lose your phone—you can go there and find out where it is right now. We can see where she is!'

So we turned to the computer. Of course the goddamned site was all in bloody German, but we have picked up enough, especially Bernadette, to stumble through the instructions. Horrible graphics, they think you like things flashing at you, but I managed to key in Sal's number and then had to dig desperately in my compost of Important Papers for the one with her Super Pin. But it could be found. In went the Super Pin, and: '*Bitte warten Sie.*' So we waited, heads close, shoulder to shoulder. Bernadette said, low, 'No matter where she is, she's still got those clothes on.' But the edge was gone. From here it was merely a case of waiting while the technology went through its paces.

On the screen now a map was descending incrementally, jerk by painful jerk. Such trashy colours, and blackly crammed with street names and arrows. And there, mid-screen, a set of concentric circles in red, which pulsed out from a point like the TV graphic for where a bomb had hit. That was it. That was where our daughter was.

Somehow it was dull knowledge, a factoid: the euro has risen against the dollar. The technology had done its stuff, now all we had to do was to go to that pulse and get her. She was in the north. Berlin is sort of splodge-shaped, perhaps a bit like a boot with its toe in the East. We lived in the lower-left corner—the heel, if you like. She was top and centre, in a district called Wedding—actually, now that I looked at it, some distance away. She had no car, couldn't drive. But just above the pulsing circles was an U-Bahn station, Osloer Strasse. 'What the hell's she doing there?' I said.

Technology makes you think that everything is just a matter of getting the blip to connect with the cursor, but one look at Bernadette's face and I saw that this was not a system error that needed a technician; a fine that could just be paid. But, at the same time, she wasn't sneering. Now there was expectation. Now she expected me to use my professional skills. It always amazes me, this, the way people see you as having skills. 'Okay, I need my phone,' I said. 'And money, and a money card and every map in the house and the charging cord for the phone, and—'

'What d'you need that for?'

'I'm just going outside and I may be some time—my passport, and hers, and my Palm, and a pen and a notebook and a torch with new batteries—'

'Oh, shut up,' she said and began making a thermos of tea.

But I did need all those things. I needed a crowbar and a skyhook and a Get Out Of Jail Free card.

Within three minutes at least some of these items had been found and I was outside in the night and stumbling towards the S-Bahn station, coat flapping as I tried to pull it over my shoulder while in urgent motion.

Chapter Twelve

Late-night trains have I think a theatrical quality—the way you step from the dark of the platform to the brightness of the carriage. They're empty, which means that your arrival really is an arrival, you get looked at—are you a threat? Or fun to play with? Or, in this case, not so empty—I was on the S-Bahn, which goes above ground, being carried along the sole of the Berlin boot to Hermannstrasse where I would change lines and, if I was lucky—it was late, getting on for last train—catch the U8 north towards Osloer Strasse. Four seats away two guys, heads down, were making growling noises over a can. It sounded like very modern music. They were big and wearing combat clobber and I found I was urgently needing to read the schematic of the transport system which was on the ceiling, half a car-length back from them. Oh, and now I saw that there was a bigger map calling to me from away at the very far end. I studied it, grateful for a distraction, my worry about Sal too big a thing to be faced.

The train rocked through the night.

As I peered at the map's spaghetti I became aware that, down to my left, in the kick-space between the seats, there was something. Cautiously, I looked. Quite small, folded in on itself, on the cold floor, lying, with huge, black, a-weight-to-lift fighting boots which were maybe pulled in so that they couldn't be seen from the aisle. Camouflage trousers, battledress jacket. Head tucked in so that the ridge of hair which made a tufty hedge across the middle of her pale skull was all that you could see; dyed bronze. Face hidden. In her arms was a small dog, hairy, a street animal, the same colour

154

as her hair. Beneath the jacket her white tee was stained and, now that I looked, ripped, so that her dirty breast was exposed. The dog was licking the nipple.

So dirty and so low.

So rock'n'roll, so punk, so contemporary-modern. So defiant, so free, so historical, so hopeless—so young and so lost and so far down. I have lived in a land of cotton, old times there are not forgotten: I have lived entirely in a land of hot showers and toast. I wanted to speak to this curled-in girl lying on the hard cold floor, cover her, give her a hundred euro; she was the child of my sixties dream, I should take her in to my home. Instead I turned away, went back up the train towards the growling of the conferencing heavies, sat with my back to her and was carried away through the night.

In the dark window beside me my profile was carried too, I was aware of it shivering there, an image of uncertainty. The air of the train was prebreathed and there appeared to be tiny dots in it which danced like pixels before my eyes. I was in a foreign place where I couldn't speak the language travelling away from my bed as the night tipped towards the hours when the world was born. I wanted my shower and toast, I wanted to be chairing a difficult meeting—oh, to be chairing a difficult meeting. But my daughter was lost somewhere on the other side of the window.

In my pocket now my phone rang.

'Where are you?'

This was Bernadette, asking the question which has made the phone companies rich. In the future, people will forfeit huge sums for the privilege of being off-line and nowhere.

'Arriving at Hermannstrasse. Hang on, I've gotta change.'

'Martin! Wait!'

But I was ignoring the phone, I could hear her inside my hand, but what I had to do now was sprint for the U-Bahn—if the last train left without me . . . As I ran I figured that I could always take a taxi. But in Berlin the taxi is miles slower, it's all the convoluted streets and historical cobblestones. So, down the half-dark stairs at a clip, the phone talking away, bottom step and bursting onto the long, cold platform as though I was about to shout 'Fire!' It was deserted. Then, preceded by a foul cloud of underground air, a train was extruded from the tunnel and I boarded and was carried away.

'Sorry,' I said to my hand, breathless.

'Where are you now?'

'Just got onto the U8, going north.'

'She's moving.'

'What?'

'The dot on the screen is moving north.'

'How d'you know?'

Dumb, I realise. But I was tired and maybe a bit scared and really I just didn't need that dot to be moving. I dug in my bag for my best map, then said, 'So where to?'

'I think she must be on a train.'

This took a moment to sink in.

'Every time I click Refresh,' said Bernadette, 'she's further north. Also on the U8. She's ahead of you—up to Lindauer Allee.'

'Okay. Well, that's, you know, a relief. It's not like she's out there in the night or something. She's, you know, on a train.' Why did I like this so much better? A train was like a house, it was a shell round her. 'Where's she headed?'

This produced a long silence.

The thought of Sally with a destination in her head which, at one-oh-five in the morning, she was proceeding towards, this was very disturbing. Sally being carried away. 'She's got those clothes on,' said Bernadette.

I kept forgetting the clothes.

To me, Sally is just a kid. But the clothes were like *The Wrong Trousers*, they were wearing her, they were carrying her off into the night.

Not *The Wrong Trousers*. Like combat boots.

Yes, now what I've got instead of the prostitute clothes are the camouflage trousers and the ripped tee and the dirty dog licking. If Sally slips away from us, that is where she will be, down on the hard floor with all the highway riders, the footpath people—living the life and sleeping on the ground. I saw now in the image of that curled-in girl the whole run-its-gamut history of the music that I have always loved. Though it wasn't music that had laid her there. It was those of us who followed it. We thought we were onto something: a mystery train to the love land.

A chain of fools. And all of our bastard children, the thing we brought into the world, sleeping on the ground.

Riding north in Berlin on an empty train, trailing your daughter, and every choice you made in your life seemed like tracks leading directly to here.

The phone spoke again. 'She's stopped,' said Bernadette.

'Where?'

'At the end station—Wittenau. She's been there ten minutes, no movement. What's she doing—I can't remember, what's there?'

'Don't think I've ever been.' Then I said, 'Ten minutes . . . The trains don't stay at the end station for ten minutes, they go off into some shed—remember that time you sat on one at Krumme Lanke, you were feeding Sandy the breast, they took you off into the dark. I think that's where she is—she's gone off into the overnight shed.'

'Why?'

What Bernadette meant was, Why d'you think that? But she knew—because the blob on her screen hadn't moved for ten minutes. What the question slithered towards was, Why d'you think she's gone off into the overnight shed, where it will be completely dark and the train will be locked and won't move until five in the morning? But these were thoughts that neither of us wanted to hear. Drunk? But when would she have got so drunk? Fallen asleep? In those clothes?

'What will you do?' said Bernadette.

And, despite myself, my heart rose. My one talent. We baby-boomers, a whole generation that knows no more than how to find the back door: look upon us and be amazed. Nevertheless I enjoyed a little epiphany of pride and optimism—during which the doors of the train parted and, heralded by a halitosis blast of platform air, a heavy entered. Spotting that we were to be alone together, he bore down on me. A night thing, tattooed, with a dark stain of ink entirely covering the neck that emerged from his collar and went thickly on up over one side of his skull, like a hood, like hardened smoke, to end in red-devil flames on the shaved dome of his crown. 'Hang on,' I said to Bernadette—leaving the phone on so she might hear what I was dealing with out here in the night. The tattoo came on. It was impressive, if only for the pain involved, which said, I did this to me, imagine what I'm prepared to do to you . . . An ear had been left free, a white question mark in the torrent of ink, and, so as to exploit your stare, the earlobe had been pierced and filled with a black rubber stopper, like the plug for a small bath. But was bath-time really the association he wanted? Now the aesthete in me was at work: No, it should have been a bullet or maybe a bloodied incisor. Oh and now I saw that he had a ring through his nose, he just wanted to be led—plus, when finally I managed to adjust my focal length, he was in fact very fat, and shortish, with red-ringed little eyes—no, this was no heavy, this was just a bit of gutter rubbish.

But he was speaking to me.

'Hey, man,' he said in American, a voice so high-pitched and thin that it was like a wheedle, a wisp that circled in the stratosphere. I waited for the inevitable hit, the open palm, but instead he smiled. It was a smile like a loaf of bread that had been caught in a downpour, it sagged at the corners and was in danger of failing completely. 'No one on the train, man,' he said, and he sat down.

He was facing me, our knees were nearly touching, in an otherwise empty train this was aggressive and, prissy, I drew back. He noticed this. He really did have tiny eyes, though they were hard to focus on because of all that ink, which was maybe the point—I once heard a playground kid shout at another, 'You've got those horrible little big little eyes!' and that is what I wanted to say to this guy, Your soul is tiny, look at the little holes it has for windows. But everything about him said, I know already.

In fact I knew better than to speak.

'I'm Eddie,' he said in that thin stratosphere wheedle, and then his gaze fell on my hand. 'Who you talking to?'

Lots of people hold their phones on trains, it's like they want always to be ready, but I saw I was cradling mine as though Bernadette was inside it. Which of course she was. 'My wife,' I said.

He leaned forward and said down towards my hand, 'This is Eddie. Goodbye, wife.'

Immediately I put the phone to my head and said, 'Be there any moment, darling.'

'Company?'

'Just, you know, the creatures of the night, how sweetly they sing.'

'Hey, that's Dracula, man,' said Eddie. His eyes were bicycle wheels, radiating wonder. Eddie was liking me—a fearsome thing. He hefted his fat a little, changed cheeks, then leaned forward, beaming. I got even more prissy. 'Hey, man,' he said, 'let's go suck your wife.' His wheels of wonder shifted to the phone. 'Lemme talk to her.'

I said to the phone, 'We're arriving. Check the website.'

'Still there.'

'You should hang up,' I said, 'she might want to ring in.'

'Ring me back,' said Bernadette and broke the connection.

Eddie had, I saw, followed this exchange like it was a trail of breadcrumbs. His eyes were like tiny suns; they sought a lock with mine, but I had been studying the little screen of the phone, finding buttons to push. The phone beeped and chirped, my virtual pet.

The voice-over of the train intoned, 'End station, Wittenau, deesa zug endet hier.' Okay, it's not deesa but I got the message: we were arriving. Decisively I swung my pack up onto my shoulder, said, 'Bye,' and strode off up the slowing train.

I put a good carriage-length between me and Eddie, stood at the doors like Fred with my finger on the Open button, pushed at the first instant, and out. I moved quickly to a set of stairs—bulbous Eddie would not, I thought, be keen on stairs—double-timed it up them, then set off along a corridor.

Every U-Bahn station has its character stuff—graphics, colour-schemes—around the platform so that you know where you've arrived. But the corridors seem universal—tiled in yellowing yellow, with harsh bulbs inside wire cages and a river of dark asphalt that seems to have been poured from a central depot, flowing in a thousand directions. I hurried. There was no one about, though the overwhelming sense, rounding every corner, was that someone was waiting. This

160

tension between no one and someone was hard on the nerves and my clock was wound already. The someone might be a troll who lived in the corridors and was hungry, or it might be Sally. I ran, sticking to the middle of the asphalt. I swung wide on corners, I was careful about the loudness of my feet, careful that I didn't miss something. But headlong.

Then I had a thought.

As I've said, thinking is not natural to me, I was distracted and immediately ran into the corner of an Instant Photo booth, hard, bruising my cheek. From beneath the booth's curtain, legs protruded. Male legs, in black denim, with broken-heeled black boots, filthy. The legs said that someone was sitting on the floor. These weren't Sally's boots, nevertheless I had to look, I peeped round the curtain, then backed off—one glimpse of Hell is enough for me, anyway, sleeping dogs, and, sure enough, she wasn't there, just some collapsed, leaking thing in the final throes.

Turning, I sprinted back through the corridors. What I'd thought was, You should have stayed on that train. Back down the steps, clatter-clatter. If you'd stayed on you would have gone to the train-garage and that's where you want to get to. I burst onto the platform. The train, having had a nice cup of tea, now began flashing its red lights. The red lights mean that the doors will no longer open. The trains are enamelled in a poisonous yellow and, because they are German, always clean and fresh-polished. This one gleamed like prize teeth; I pounded on it. But it pulled out anyway, leaving me there, panting, on the mile of empty platform which stretched away like despair at either hand.

Stepping from behind a pillar, Eddie said, 'Hi, darling.'

I don't think I've gone on enough about Eddie's voice. It was like the whistle from a kettle, like the wheek of a gate. He was a squeaker, a stuck pig. His eyes seemed for some reason

161

to have contracted to pinheads, his needle-gaze pricked everything. He stood in front of me, not exactly blocking my way, and said, 'Find her?'

He was fishing and we both knew it. But his pinpricks said he'd caught something in my eyes. He came closer, smiling his wet-bread smile, and said, 'Let's go.' This was produced so happily—Eddie was as friendless as they come and now he thought he was going to hold my hand. Fred says that, 'Let's go, Dad,' it's so simple, it's designed to make you think that this was previously agreed. Fred, Fred, sprawled in his bed. Sandy lying next to Mummy. The warmth of the blankets and the sound of night breathing heard down the hall—all of this was what I longed for.

Instead I had Eddie. I looked at him, hard, and said, 'Okay, where to?'

'I dunno, man.'

I summoned all the ugly I could find and said, 'I'm gonna beat the crap out of you, Eddie.'

'Okay, man,' said Eddie. And that smile came again, hanging slack off his cheekbones. He didn't back away even an inch and I knew that Eddie had faced down playground nasties for all of his thirty years. To hit, I saw this, he would be like Mr Blobby, always coming back up smiling.

But I was wasting time.

I turned sharply, went off up the platform. It was as long as a runway, dim-lit, dull-coloured, a vast slab of meatloaf cooling down for the night. I found yellow rubbish bins to look in, glowing adverts to look behind, cold rows of mesh-metal seats, all empty. Beer cans on their sides like fallen pillars. I went all the way to one end and came back up the other side, checking the ceilings, looking into the trough where the tracks ran. Nothing. Mid-point I passed Eddie, at the foot of the stairs, turning slowly so that his eyes were always on mine. The only way out of here, he knew, were those stairs and so why waste his breath? All the way up to the other end I went, a glance into the paired tunnels, dark nostrils, then, as though I was on an elastic, back to Eddie. Home to Mum.

As I approached I saw that he was going to speak to me and I couldn't stand the thought, he knew I was fucked, he had me, so just to piss him off I kept going past the stairs and along the platform. It was sheer cussedness, there was nowhere for me to go but I went anyway, just to see his suck-hole of a mouth fall open. All the way to the far end of the platform, and then I had another idea.

I dropped to the track and began to walk into the arch of the left-hand tunnel. This is where my train had gone. Was this dangerous? I really didn't know. There were the two rails, gleaming, and then a third over on the far, non-platform side. I had always presumed this was the power track and, stepping from sleeper to sleeper, I kept parallel to it, one shoulder hunched as though I was afraid it would snake up and bite me. On into the blackness—I could see the rails shining as they ran to a point and, far ahead, the red eye of a signal light. I had a torch but I didn't want to use it yet—Eddie might follow a torch. From the platform I heard his squeak, 'Hey, man,' as forlorn as the whistle of a prairie train, 'Hey, don't go in there, man, there's a thing in there—did you see *By Night They Come*? That thing with all the cockroaches coming out of its mouth, that's where it lives, man. Hey, man. Hey . . .' Eddie squeaking behind me was just what I didn't need, I was trying to listen, for a train, for the thing. Between the sleepers was gravel and my feet crunched, loud in the tunnel's acoustics. For Sally's sound. That was it: there were so many sounds, my heartbeat drumming in my ears, and somewhere water was dripping, a smell of bricky damp, and that red light burning ahead, but what I was really listening out for was Sally.

And what exactly would Sally's sound be? Her partying with some Kraut louts? Or singing a lonesome-girl-lost song, a bit drunk and solo and waiting for the dawn? No. It would be the sound of her being forced.

Yes, a number of the uglier elements were, like the train tracks, coming to a focal point ahead of me in that tunnel. But as I took each crunchy step, what added the poison to the mix was the thought that I was walking into the primal bodily moment of Sally's life. The thought of what I was going to see rose inside me like the warm airs of death as you approach a carcass—a rotten sheep in a hollow, going right up your nose. What added the poison was the knowledge that I had brought this to her—go on, Martin, take a good whiff.

What are your expectations for your daughter's first sex? Well, you're not supposed to think about it, are you, it's a kind of incest. Or else you think good thoughts: of course she will be the initiator, girls can do anything, and with some golden-haired boy-poet who is rather thoughtful and shy, highly intelligent, and sensitive, but not soft, and, because she loves him, she will . . . in a pig's eye. The back of a car, or on the boards of a porch, fumbly and hurried, the guy desperate to keep going in case she changes her mind. And it never did us any harm. Did it.

Anyway, not that, not for Sally. Not even that.

And I was going to see it.

Now the phone rang. It didn't give any little warning shudder, I wasn't thinking about it, and it rang, right there in the tunnel, and I just about jumped on the electric rail.

'Bernadette?'

'Where are you now?'

'Walking along the train tracks. In a tunnel going to the overnight shed. Has she moved?'

'No.'

I had stopped walking to talk and now on the phone there was a silence. Then Bernadette said, 'Maybe you should wait?'

No, I should get there and put a stop to—but I didn't say that.

'The police said to wait.'

'Ah.'

'I had to, Martin.'

'Of course.'

There was another silence and this time its subject was the hundred thousand—in whatever mind's eye Bernadette and I, husband and wife, had in common, there now appeared a suitcase full of money only to begin at once upon shrinking, getting smaller and smaller until it was a tiny dot, like a full stop, with a puff of smoke rising from it. That little dot was full of a surprisingly sharp pain—I heard myself go 'Ouff.' The hundred thousand had had all kinds of escapes in it and now the sense of being in jail for life was a dead weight to the limbs. Instead of escape there was going to be an unpleasant interlude with the police while I explained my urgent need to be in the Nigerian Embassy, followed by an interlude in a German prison cell. I saw myself sitting forlornly on a cold wooden bench in striped overalls, my head in my hands. Close-cropped hair and splattered in the shit of pigeons that had come home to roost. All of that passed between us in an instant. Oh, great marriage of true minds, to have brought us such gifts. Then Bernadette, being less of a wallower, said, 'Don't wait. Martin?'

'No, darling, I won't.' And with the phone still pressed to my ear I started again to walk towards the red light. I had a hand up to shield one eye, the other was on that power track, in case it tried to get me—from sleeper to sleeper I went, so as to reduce the crunching, making me lengthen my stride, which meant I was getting there quicker. Which was the aim, wasn't it.

'Are you there?'

'Yes, here, darling. Sorry, it's hard to walk and talk in the dark.'

I kept on striding, waiting to hear what she'd say. She didn't say anything. But she was with me. I strode on, keeping her at my ear. Our marriage, for better or worse. And here was the light at the end of the tunnel, except that it was red. Red for danger. Red for Hell. Red for blood—red light on everything like a butcher's window. 'I better go,' she said.

'In case she rings in.'

'Yes.'

'Bye.'

'Bye, darling. Be careful.' And she rang off.

But what did she mean, Be careful? That she was worried, sure. But the way she'd said it said she was worried about me. And Sally, of course. But me too. Was that right? I felt a little surge of happiness and, as happiness always does, it made me feel a little weak. There in the night rail-yard of the U-Bahn I had a little surge of happiness that I was loved by my wife.

Tides of cheap emotion surging through me.

Now, beyond the tunnel, the tracks spread out like a delta, when finally I had the red light behind me I could see their metal gleam—which one to take? Ahead was a low shed, with a roof that spread wide like the wings of a gliding bird, and along its front were eight openings. In each opening was a train, a bullet inside a barrel. I was making pictures, I couldn't help it—maybe this was to prevent the appearance

166

of the one picture I could not bear to make. Yes, an image was pressing at the edge of my vision and I thrust it away: be methodical, I told myself, and I headed towards the left-hand end. Then I stopped. The trains were right there, I should listen, maybe I would hear her. I put a hand to my ear.

Distant cars. A faraway siren. Above, the stars twinkling uselessly.

Nothing.

Not just any old nothing. This was a silence that told me, She isn't here. Nothing is here, just trains. Just useless stuff. Only people matter, the rest is just stuff. Well, yeah, we all know that. But life has to put a gun to our heads before we'll admit it.

But I had to look and so, a walking pillar of uselessness, I trudged across the night to the left-hand train. Up close, it was high and I realised that usually when I was next to a train I was standing on a platform. Its bright, yellow-painted flank gleamed hard, impenetrable. From down around my ankles came a smell of oil and metal. From the shed itself, a nose-full of musty brick. This was a dead place, or at least sleeping. Nothing, utterly nothing. But I had to look and so I climbed the metal steps which got the driver up to his door and, clinging onto the door-handle, swung out, leaning in so that I could see into the interior of the carriage.

In my mind I had planned that this interior was going to be bright-lit. But the train was dead, there was only the darkness of a room inside a sleeping house. As I shone my torch through the window and peered, still holding on with one stretched hand to the door-handle, leaning, with my nose against the cold glass, a feeling of complete pointlessness came over me. There were eight trains, and each train had maybe ten carriages, and I could not really see properly even into this first one.

Chapter Thirteen

The metal steps that the driver went up to get to the cab were perforated, like a doily—I sat down on one and tried to think. What could I do? To search all eighty carriages would take a couple of months. What if I walked alongside them, very slowly, used all my senses—wait until I bristled? Like dowsing, except that I'm not the dowsing kind. But maybe I could try? Wouldn't I smell something? Sex smells very strongly; blood also. Or hear some tiny sounds, moaning, breathing even. If someone was inside this carriage, would I hear them? Maybe not consciously. But I am a great believer in the beneath-conscious power of the senses. Wasn't I in a hyper-alert state?

Way back, we believed that you knew everything if only you knew how to know.

I lowered myself to the ground and turned my back on the opening to the night. Above me, the hard yellow flank of the carriage ran away into the greater gloom of the interior. I stared into the darkness. It was in darkness, I knew, that the primeval self could walk. I opened the door in my chest and tried to encourage that naked thing to emerge. My ears seemed like caves, echoey. Slowly I drew in the deepest breath. I could taste the way that hot electricity had burned the metal brushes which dragged on the power rail. I caught the smell of the rats that lived in the rafters. Like a rifleman, I tried to slow my heartbeat. The top of my head began to tingle. Yes, yes—I was connecting. Thus, when the phone went off in my pocket my head jerked and banged hard against the side of the train.

My fingers, crackling with sensitivity, wrestled with the dumb fabric of my pocket. I got the thing in my hand, stabbed Yes, and banged it to the side of my already-banged head. 'What?' I said.

'She's alive!'

'What? Oh . . . oh.' And I sank onto the carriage's metal step and waited while a spasm of sobbing worked its way through me.

'Martin?'

I said, 'Did you call off the police?'

'Yes.'

'Great. Oh, *great!*' And I let out a long sigh. Now, in the little theatre which plays behind my eyes a truly amazing thing was to be seen. The curtains swished apart and, on the bare boards of the stage, a tiny dot, a mote, was caught by a spotlight beam and began to grow, sucking into itself all the other motes, sucking from the air around it despair, frustration, my loser's history and, while I watched, swelled into a suitcase, the lid of which rose gracefully to reveal euros in neatly-bound bundles to the value of exactly one hundred thou. Now I saw, on the stage, a scene soft-lit by faded sunlight where to the strains of *San Francisco Wear Some Flowers In Your Hair* my children paddled in the shallows of a great, gentle ocean, while, beneath crimson heads of pohutukawa, Bernadette and I walked hand in hand . . .

'Tell me,' I said to her. There was a grin spreading on my face.

'She rang in.'

'And?'

'She's alive.'

'Well, she would be, wouldn't she.'

'Well . . .'

There was a silence and I felt myself tense. The lid of the

suitcase began to close. 'What d'you mean?'

'I don't know . . . She didn't—it's just, she didn't sound very good.'

'Where is she? What'd she say?'

'She wants you to come and get her. You. She asked for you and I said you were out looking for her and she said you should come and get her. In a taxi. Fast, she said.'

'Okay, fine. What's the problem?'

'I don't know.'

'But there is one?'

'Might be. She wouldn't say. She's on someone else's handy, I have the number. But she told me not to ring.'

'What?' I straightened, walked out of the engine shed, and stood in the night between the tracks. Looking up, my head was again tingling, as though connections were making themselves. What was this? My eyes observed the stars and the moon—gibbous, I thought dimly, registering the use of the never-needed word.

'She called me Bernadette.'

'Bernadette.'

'Yes, like that. She said everything carefully.'

'That sounds quite bad,' I said. There was between us a long silence of agreement. 'I better go,' I said, and I started to walk briskly back along the track towards the red light. 'Give me the number.' I stopped, wrote it on the back of my hand, checked it. Horrible writing, but the characters glowed like a miracle code, that could keep Sally alive. 'Where is she?'

'Bildenburger Strasse. She said she was outside Bildenburger Strasse 32.'

'Outside it?'

'In Oranienberg.'

*

170

Back through the tunnel I ran. It was possible, I knew, that when you were running between train tracks in the middle of the night and the sleepers were placed far apart you might fall and land on the power line, and be vaporised. Nevertheless I ran. I had stowed the phone in my pocket, it was thumping against my side as though it had a point to make. Think, think, I was telling myself, think, I said it so hard that it made thinking impossible. So her phone's on the train but she's in Oranienberg—okay, so she and her phone were separated. Okay—thump, thump, run. She's on someone else's phone and she's talking carefully—so someone is with her? Run, run, stumble. Someone who wants me to come, too—so not a rapist.

Not a murderer. Not a boy she's running away with.

As I burst out of the tunnel and clambered up onto the platform I thought, Bloody Oranienberg—it's bloody miles.

So why doesn't she want anyone to ring?

My feet slapped loudly in the silence of the platform. I slowed, it was as though to make a noise here was to risk waking something and, sure enough, here was gatekeeper Eddie, floating blimp-like into view, tattoo shocking me all over again, his pinwheels all wheeling like crazy. 'Hey, Action Man,' he squeaked, 'where to now?'

I slowed as though I was going to parley with him, then accelerated up the stairs, double-time. I could feel the pinwheels on my back, searching for purchase. He called, 'I saw her!'

Turning, I was two flights above him and I looked down through the oblong case of the stairway. Our eyes met, measured. His face turned slightly, bringing the inky side into play—it was as though he wanted to hide his emptiness behind the flames. 'Bye, Eddie,' I said, and ran on.

Through the corridors of the upper levels. From the Instant

171

Photo booth the dead legs continued to protrude. These stations are like the levels of Paradise, you have to work your way up through them. Along the walls now were those who hadn't made it, long figures shrouded in newspapers. Their animals eyed me. More stairs, up I went—this was *Tomb Raider*, but the reality-TV version. I passed a scabby group arguing about Spinoza, in unison they turned and extended a pietà of open hands. I was chased by a stud-collared dog. But nothing could touch me, the gun was to my head and only people mattered to me now, not these underworld things, and I burst from the stairs and out into the openness of the night. 'Taxi!'

Climbed in. Ahhh . . .

German taxis are a reflection of all that is good about this troubled nation. The world should do itself a favour and get German taxis to go global; I have never had a bad one. For a start they're all Mercedes Benz's, none of your dent-mobiles, and they're always clean. I imagine the Inspector of Taxi Hygiene to be a busy man. He will have a clipboard and a moustache—I once put the moustache-quotient of a Sachsenhausen meeting at eighty percent. There is probably an Inspector of Taxi-Driver Moustaches. Imagine being his Assistant and having to present your upper lip for inspection every morning. Imagine being his wife. But I digress.

It's the relief.

The driver wanted a Kaution, Oranienberg being bloody miles—fortunately this was a word I knew, they make you pay a deposit when you rent an apartment, so I gave him a fifty-euro note to look after and that produced an atmosphere of sweetness and light. I gave him the address, which he repeated and then said, 'Alles klar,' all is clear, which always reminds me of the way that Scientologists say they want to go clear—and the taxi moved off, like a ship of dreams. The driver was playing light classics, Mantovani, I'd say, and I sank back into a velvet cushion of violins and let everything trickle out of my head.

But Oranienberg is just a nice way of saying Sachsenhausen, it means watch-towers and gas and experiments on bodies, the work I have to complete before we can go home, it's not a place I wish ever to be bound for, but I am, carried on black tyres spinning faster by the second, we were moving onto the open road, headlights finding the white line and mixed now with those ghastly historical images was Sally. It has happened, finally: the Holocaust and my family in the same sentence. I couldn't speak its language but I had at last entered Germany.

I rang Bernadette. 'Any calls?'

'Nothing. Where are you?'

'Taxi.' The white line came in instalments, pieces of a stripe that was being shot towards my eyes. 'Tell me, why didn't she want anyone to ring her?'

'Didn't say.'

'What did she say, actually?'

'*Don't ring me—tell him to get here*. That's all.'

'Okay.' So I consulted the back of my hand, and then dialed.

This is modern life, see. These little machines with arrows inside them—what I see is arrows arcing out of these phones, curving round the globe, falling like the deadly rain from a company of archers, and can you avoid it? Soon we'll all have the same haircuts, we'll be walking stock options, and it's these little machines: trust me on this. If only we had been allowed to run the world . . . In my ear there was the ringing tone. The phone's little blue screen would, I knew, be saying *Connecting*, promising everything. But as usual there was only a recorded message, as usual in German. So she had turned the mailbox on, or someone had. I half-listened; there was a beep and I knew I was supposed to be recording. I rang off. But then as the black tyres spun and the German, after the usual little delay, sorted itself out in my head, I got it that the recorded message had been female but that in the middle a male voice had spoken, had said a word: Günter.

I dialed again, and then again, and listened to this Günter say his name. Dark and growly. A smoker's voice. Fifty—well, forty at least—anyway, four times her age. This was what she was with. What had they done together? Okay, I knew that. The facts are basic, it's the same in-out all over the planet. But how did it go? It's like the human face, two eyes, one mouth, but the variations are infinite and utterly fascinating to us. How was it? What was it? What did it make you into, when you were in it? What are you now? That's what I asked myself: what is she now?

The taxi paused beneath a motorway light while the driver consulted a map. 'Bildenburger Strasse,' I said. Picture-Citizen Street.

'Alles klar,' he chimed, and we were off again.

I used to think that it was work that the sixties were about. No more turning up every day in the worn suit to put in the forty hours; the forty years. Now work was going to be play and we would all be players. But now I see that it was about sex. Was there a single song about being married? Actually, I can think of two and they're both downers. I used to think the idea was that we would play at running the world, brilliantly. Now what I see is how we instinctively knew there was no longer going to be any sex once you were married. That's it. The sixties were about staying sexed-up.

This guy I know, let's call him John, once turned up with his wife of a decade, let's say Susan, this was in a wine bar just a couple of years back, and announced with immense gusto,

174

'Susan and I had this brilliant fuck in the weekend. It was amazing! It went on for hours! It was, oh—totally amazing!' The sight of people needing right now to be somewhere else, anywhere but our table, was instant, all you could see was backs. Oh, and Susan's face, which was a strawberry. John is one of those guys who prides himself on never having fallen. Gusto is everything; hair still just down over the collar.

You can read it on any website, it's everywhere these days: marriage is the end of sex. Said, sure, with a kind of rueful giggle. With brisk worldliness; with compassionate bluntness. But said. And somehow—this is the message—that is how it should be. Marriage—or is it families? Yes, that's what I see now, how the sixties tried to end families so that sex wouldn't die. Yes: how being in the hot of fucking was the primal moment when all the grim of the world was banished to the far end of the rainbow—and so fucking had to be kept hot forever.

And if the grim comes into sex?

I saw now the waif-girl on the train—as the taxi sped, her train sped beside me, and I could look down upon her, lying curled-in between the seats and still.

If this Günter has been in Sally, will she start her life in a world dead to love? I made a bargain with myself, with fate: if Sally had come through this okay then I would devote myself to her.

As the taxi streamed me, all this was going off in my head. As I was streamed, on spinning black wheels, towards Sally in her moment, I knew that the hole in the heart of my thinking had opened. That I, and she, and everything that was good in the little world that Bernadette and I had scrambled together, was now falling through.

*

Now the taxi is off the inter-city and working its way through urban streets again. Houses, houses, and in every one a member of the jury that will convict me. Yes, with every house we are coming closer to the moment when I will have to confront what I have done. I feel grim, a kind of grim desperation that makes me determined to focus on practicalities and my hand goes into the deep pocket of my backpack for the Swiss Army Knife. In the darkness down behind the driver's seat I lever out the longest blade and test its edge with my thumb. The thought of my hand pressing this length into someone's body is so ghastly that a nasty taste comes up into my mouth. At the same time I have to fight the urge to laugh. Who do I think I am? Nevertheless, when I return the knife to the bag the blade is still out—I try to stand the knife handle-up so that if I have to grab it and use it I can do so quickly.

We're slowing; the driver looks at me in the mirror. 'Nummer swanzish,' I say, number twenty. Beneath a street light, we settle up. I get a receipt. Why? Who am I going to claim this from, Stevens? The thought gives me a hundred thousand euros worth of pain. But the receipt will prove I was here, when I came, the number of the cab. Suddenly I'm thinking evidence, police. Then I am standing on the footpath in the cool of the night air and the taxi is doing a u-turn. I see he's watching to see where I'll go at, what is it, 2:28 in the morning, and slowly I turn and proceed towards the gate of the nearest house. I am somewhat in shock at being out in the night, bereft of the cosiness of the cab. Then he's gone and I break off and start walking up Bildenburger Strasse.

If this was Berlin the street would be lined by a high wall of apartment buildings but here the houses are actual houses, each with its own garden and fence. It's a no-parking street, the kerb is clear and I can see a long way, up to where number

32 must be. Nothing. Outside it, she said. I peer into the blotchy glare thrown by the street lighting. I stop and listen (shouldn't I be hurrying?). In this sleepy place there is only the sound of sleep. I stand so long that my feet get sore. Nothing. But I wouldn't call it peaceful. As the silence deepens what you get is the under-sounds, the ones that rise from within. Groaning—the bodies of Sachsenhausen, rising to have their say. The agony of Iraq, the war-song of Rumsfeld and co, it's as though it all enters the world precisely at the point where I am standing. I can't stay there and I make myself start to walk.

Not long now—number 27. The houses are close on either side and they are so regularly spaced that they form a sort of canyon, which I am going up the middle of. I realise I am tiptoeing and I make myself walk. I make myself cough, experimentally. The sound lingers.

Number 30 and, even in the shadowy light, from here I can see, surely, anything that would be outside number 32—and there's nothing. Is she hiding in a bus stop somewhere? There is a bus stop, but it's a hundred metres further along and on the wrong side of the road. I am trying to shout her name but somehow I just can't. Surely the only element I have is surprise? Now I really am tiptoeing, number 31, the feeling is like going into the underground room at Sachsenhausen, holding yourself against what might come next, and then here it is, 32, a square two-storey brick house, standing in darkness, with its windows shuttered, and window boxes, and a little garden, which, in the blotchy light, looks to be all lumpy shadows. So is she down in one of the shadows? I am peering over the fence when there is a noise.

To my left, standing quietly, is a car—an Audi, I see the four rings of the logo, note them for evidence, and the colour of the car, which is dark, maybe dark green. Then, studying,

I realise that I can't see into it because it has blacked-out windows. The car is standing still and cold there in the night and it had seemed irrelevant, just a thing, like cut-out shape with no meaning. Now I am understanding that, in the driveway, it is, yes, outside number 32.

Now, in the same way that you understand German a delayed moment after it was spoken, I am working out what the noise was: the electric lock of the doors of the car being worked. I stare at the car and feel everything in me rise as though I am going to have to make a huge leap. Its bloody darkened windows mean that nothing can be seen inside. Darkened windows, they're for wankers, and instantly I know everything about Günter and my hand goes to the knife in the pocket of the backpack and seizes the handle. At the same time, in my coat pocket, my phone rings. I just leave it. But the ringing is simply terrible, it's so loud and it's calling attention to me when all attention should be on that car. Inside the pocket my thumb finds Yes and I push, which ends the ring. But now Bernadette's voice can be heard in there, squeaking to get out. I don't answer. I just leave the line open. Hands in pockets, I'm standing at the gateway, at the boot of the Audi, as though I'm fishing for my keys. Then, slowly, the front door on the right-hand side—the passenger's side— swings open, as though someone, from inside, has given it a push. It's a heavy door. As it swings, the interior light goes on inside the car, the shape of the door-opening is outlined. But, because of the wanky darkened windows I can't see a thing in there. In my pocket Bernadette's voice keeps demanding to be put in the picture and I just let it. The door hangs, heavy in the night. I wait. Nothing, absolutely nothing. So I make myself take a step towards it.

Chapter Fourteen

I have the knife out now and hidden down by my side. It is utterly dumb, a person like me with a knife and I wish someone else was doing this—someone qualified. I'm close along the flank of the car but I can't see. I make myself take the one step, but that isn't enough. I wait. But nothing continues to happen. All around me in the dark are long shadows, the house, the trees, which loom, but there's no sound. Then I hear, from inside the car, a little grunt, as though someone is shifting their weight. Such a human sound, but what does it mean? So I rise to my tiptoes and almost fall into the next step. I'm going to look. The knife is clenched tightly. In my left-hand pocket Bernadette has gone quiet but I know she's listening too. The step carries me into a second step, I put one hand on the roof of the car and I do this with just a little more of a slap than is necessary, so as to make a sound. It's a contradiction, I know, to tiptoe and then announce your presence, but that's what I did. Then I start to lean down. I don't want to lean in, somehow I want my face to be as far away as possible from whatever it is that's in there, but the car is low and I don't want to squat, I want to be ready to spring away. So I thrust my face forward and make myself see.

Blood.

At first I don't see what is under the blood. It's splattered on the dash, on the seat covering, on the high boots of black leather. Dribbles, spots, thick pools—blood has covered everything and changed its nature. Its smell goes right up my nose. We all know the state of blood, it's a universal area of human expertise—old and dry, wet and still running,

179

the thickness of it, we know all this at a glance. But what we never see is a lot. This is all of it. This is a gout from a great wound, a fatal wound—drying. Under the blood is a person.

There is blood in her hair, great hanging gobs of it. It is set into a mask on her face—it is impossible to see her face. I don't recognise her, I can't, but I have seen the boots. A thick coat of red all down the tight blouse—one glance and I know that I am seeing most of eight pints.

I can't recognise her, I can't. The face is held stiffly. But then the eyes in it come round, slowly, in that stiff-masked face, held by the grip of the dry blood, to meet me.

Her eyes were older than mine. It was like looking into the eyes of a tomb painting that have watched while thousands of years have come and gone.

I open my mouth to say her name but those eyes stop me. Slowly, stiffly, she starts to get out of the car. There is a sort of tearing sound as her clothes come away from the seat—they're stuck, but she pulls determinedly. I stand back, respectful. Finally she is standing clear of the car. In the boots she's taller. Then the eyes catch mine and, with just the slightest movement, they indicate that I am required to look inside. So down I go. My jaw is out, I can feel the clench of my teeth. The camera of my head dollies down and in. The seat coverings are pale and in the right-hand seat I can see the shape where Sally's body has been, left clean, though a fresh drip is starting to run down through it. Absurdly, I want to wipe this away. Finally, I make myself look further. How bad can it be? After all, she's alive and functioning. There's going to be someone dead, I know that—so how bad can it be? And there is. It's Günter. Behind the steering wheel, he's well-dressed in a trashy sort of way, with a silk scarf that was once white. Apart from the scarf there doesn't seem to be so much red on him. A bit. But the fight has gone out of him and his face is drained—bloodless—and is never going to be any other colour. His eyes are open—he is seeing what the tomb paintings see. His body has shrunk somehow, as though something has been sucked out of it. His lips are parted. In his neck there is a wound and in the wound there is a knife.

Sally indicated with her eyes that I should close the door of the car. I was about to give it a boot—I wasn't in control—but her eyes stopped me. Looking at her, getting her approval, I pushed it slowly with my fingertips until it was just about to click, when her chin gave a little movement. The light inside the car had gone out—enough. I stopped. Her chin was jutted, even under all the blood I could see that.

She turned and, in the high-heeled black boots, walked slowly off the property. I followed. I wanted to ask, What happened? I can't tell you how massively these words came inside me—despite everything, I had a primal curiosity that I had to satisfy. I was ashamed of this and tried to suppress it. And I wanted to say her name; even more: I wanted to use her name to make a connection between us, to return her to herself—to put us back into our selves. And this she was not going to have.

At the kerb she paused, then crossed the road and, jerky, began to walk down the other side. Her heels were loud. It was a sound that took me back to the Nigerian Embassy, where, just hours before, I had hid in the dark, on this very day, and when I realised that I let out a sob. She heard and she turned and put her face on me and after that there were no more sobs.

Ahead of me now she made a shape in the night out of

181

a noir classic. She was a femme fatale and I was the king of the night who would follow her on to a torrid scene which would drag me down to my lusted-for doom. There were long expressionist shadows and puddles with significant reflections. But that was all shit. I tagged along behind my daughter who was forty years younger than me and knew that everything inside my head was dumb shit out of a movie.

Behind the bus shelter she lay down on her back and waited for me to come to her. The shelter was mostly glass, it wouldn't hide much if a car came past, but I saw that there was nowhere else. She was lying on the hard concrete. I knelt over her. Again I started to say her name but she wasn't having any. Her lips moved under the mask of blood. 'Wash me.'

There were puddles in the gutter. I carried water from them, splashed her cheeks and neck, rubbed. Down on my knees, trying to get the red matter out of her hair. 'The boots,' she said.

At the puddles, the backs of my hands scraped against the raw surface of the road as I tried to cup as much water as possible. I pressed my hands together tightly as I walked, trying to carry without spilling. Devotion to these tasks was a relief. I washed her hands and arms and her knees and legs, right up to where the tiny mini-skirt, now with a broad, dark streak down the middle of it, began. Then, without warning, she stood up. She tottered in the boots, then righted herself, and shook the long black leather coat off her shoulders. She used it to dry herself as best she could—those parts of its lining that weren't soaked. She put a fresh smear of red on her cheek and I went for more water. Without the coat she hardly had any clothes on and what she had were wet, she was shivering. I took off my coat and hung it on her shoulders and she wrapped herself in it.

Now she looked at the leather coat and said, 'Put it in the car.'

Had there been just a tiny acknowledgement in her voice that this was upside-down, her giving orders to me? I tried a smile but she definitely wasn't having any. Bundling the coat, I held it away from me and returned to number 32. In my hands it was heavy, wet, I could feel the wet getting on me. I opened the door and threw it in.

And there, maintaining his position beneath the warm interior light of the Audi, was Günter. He was still dead, still an empty human body, a body that had been drained of life, and now he was part of my family, and was forever going to be. I wanted to speak to him, to say how sorry I was about all this. I won't pretend I suddenly thought he was a nice guy. It wasn't, I imagined, too hard to figure: he threatened Sally with a knife and then had it used on him. I gagged a little as, in his presence, I realised the probable truth of this—that Sally had killed a man with a knife—and even though I was staring right at the evidence I just could not take it in. I could not accept it. But the angle of the blade was right: Sally was right-handed, her stab would have come from the right and below, and caught him, in middle age, in a droopy moustache, with his hair permed into an immaculate silver-flecked cloud around his head, and a silk scarf, and the thin gold chain of a little medallion around his neck. Leather jacket, dark trousers with a discreet stripe, heeled boots. Now I saw that the knife had a little ivory on its handle, it was probably some kind of a joke-knife, a switchblade bought for showing off, for picking his teeth with. I know, I know, I'm forgiving this guy and he was undoubtedly a rapist and got what he deserved. But, looking at him in the frozen gore of his death-scene—Günter, this was your life—I understood. What was in him was also in me.

Chapter Fifteen

The events of the night unfolded slowly and then in turn were followed by the events of the month that followed. Sally came home with me, we called the police, who, considering that a man had been stabbed to death, were remarkably sympathetic. There were some tricky moments—where are these clothes of leather coming from? Was I that man who has been interviewed with Herr Stevens several nights ago in Erdmann-Graeser-Weg? So in which place Herr Stevens is right now?—but nothing that couldn't be handled. Sally was given two weeks off school with more to come if necessary, during which time there was an inquest of sorts and some media interest, but, again, the police were helpful and in fact protective. Nothing that couldn't be handled. The German media are more considerate; it is on the whole a considerate country, knowing as it does what it means to have been through something; I guess I've been a bit cavalier about that. Bernadette took the chance, with Sally to babysit, to get everything packed, and then they were gone. Nothing much had changed, really. We still had Sally. We still loved each other. Sandy was till cute.

Fred cried at the airport, he couldn't look at me, and then he made himself and his eyes were huge with tears. He smiled bravely. It kills me, kids being brave. He waved, they all waved, in the end even Sally waved, once, and I waved back. Afterwards, I took a taxi direct to Potsdamer Platz and sat through a movie. Then a taxi home. That made three taxis for the day, bloody expensive, but it's not every day that you and so forth, and it's only money. I went straight to bed and thus it wasn't until morning that I woke to the empty house.

This empty house. I've been through the dirty-dishes-in-piles phase, the pizza phase, the hours-on-the-couch-with-the-remote phase—thirty-seven channels keeps you going for a while. Okay, I looked at some porn sites, I admit it, but it was only once. Also the late-night porn on the TV, of course I did, but it's so lame. It's so grim, even if you've had a few, which was also a phase. Especially if you've had a few. No more movies. Usually I would go to every movie but not right now.

The facts of Sally's case, when stripped down, turned out to be very simple. She set off in her clothes to do a look-at-me twirl for a girl from school, met Günter on the train and was charmed. She got excited and lost her phone. Got into his car to go to a nightclub. Found she seemed to be leaving the city and complained. Then raged, then screamed, but the car had central locking and darkened windows. In Bildenburger Strasse he'd shown her the knife and then put it on the seat between them, as though it was only a warning device, symbolic. His handy had rung and while he was taking the call she had seen her chance.

That simple.

That simple, that tidy. That sequential. Sequence: now there was a subject that I began to spend some time on. As Fred had once told me, the news is followed by the weather.

Sally who was followed by Fred who was followed by Sandy, whose cord I had cut. Wendy in Standard Two who was followed by Sandra who I had kissed in the school play; Frances who was followed by Linda who was followed by Bronwyn who was followed by Mary; who was followed by Christine who was followed by Maureen who was followed by Alison who was followed by my first wife. Obviously there is the odd name missing in there; I'm working on that.

185

Then Kerry, Marion, a couple of nameless ones, then Briar, then Judy. And then Bernadette. Or sometimes it would be jobs. Or beds I had slept in. I knew from my Memorial work that the problem with chronological presentations of history is that the roots of one period inevitably lie further back than the period immediately preceding, unquote. Followed is one thing; led-to quite another. For example: did Sally's being on that train lead to the phone call that Bernadette took from the police while I was in the taxi going out to Oranienberg? 'Dear Frau Rumsfield, does your daughter have a little dog and also a dog collar with spikes around her neck? No. That is good; auf Wiedersehen.' This I followed up and discovered that a homeless teenage girl had been found dead on a U8 train. She'd been missing for four months from a town called Obertrubach, which is in the south, I looked it up, in Franconia. Her name was Angelika Strube. She will always be in our family now, too. So was it causality that meant I would always know her name and hometown or was this just random? You decide.

Of course I continued to work on the facilitation required by the problem of Sachsenhausen. But my associates there were aware of my circumstances and were all very considerate. They no longer looked to me for a solution to the problem. The ongoing situation. I was now merely another colleague, a fellow attendee at the meetings; one of course to be listened to with deference and politeness, if ever I should say anything.

I made myself spend time down at the lake. Did the near-drowning, which after all had now been forty-two years ago, signal the start of the sequence which had brought me here to this cold wedge of ground at the water's edge? A logic could be constructed. Meanwhile the water continued to call to me. You could just swim out, it said. Leaves floated on its

186

surface, fish rose, when it was raining its surface was covered in dimples which were attractive to the contemplative eye.

'Random!'

Stevens, calling collect from Brighton—that's Brighton, England, which is not in Africa. Three months had passed, a very long time; whatever had happened to Sally he figured I was over it, right?

'Long way from Nigeria, Stevens.'

'Fucken Nigeria, don't get me started, the fucken Nigels have taken over Nigeria, man, it's quiche-eaters wall to wall out there. Total bummer. But, Random, my man, it's a relief, man—good ol' Random. Ever been to Brighton? It's a great scene, man. Listen: how soon can you get over?'

'It's raining here, Stevens, sorry, I don't think I could venture out right now.'

'Listen, Random, get serious with me, man, this is like the hugest opportunity, man—I've met this guy down here, Random, listen to this: he's Pinkie.'

Stevens figured correctly that I would know who Pinkie of Brighton was, he gave me time to be impressed. I said, 'The original, right? The original Pinkie.'

'Exactly, man—how cool is that? Have you ever read that book—he gave me a signed copy! Listen, man, I need you. I'm starting something serious here, I need like five operatives, pronto—how quickly can you get here, man?'

'Sorry, there was some rain falling on the line just then, I don't think I caught that.'

'Random . . . Man . . .' There was a long pause—if you listened it really did sound like it was raining on the line. Then he said, 'Give me a break, man.'

Gently, I put down the phone.

It fact it *was* raining. I took an umbrella and set off for the lake. It was very cold, on the concrete path my feet produced a faint crackling. I needed a coat. But I had become used to not wearing one. It was as though I was keeping myself cold—as though I needed to be cooled down.

At the lake the gardeners had obeyed the annual clock and removed the bench seat, into storage for winter—because who would ever want to sit out here when the lake wasn't for swimming? I went to the end of the little jetty and looked down. It was early evening, and dark. The lake was frozen; where there used to be water, now there was something that looked like you could walk on it—this was a kind of miracle. From the jetty I looked down into the white frozen hardness of it and saw bubbles of air trapped in the ice. It wasn't hard to imagine a tiny world inside each bubble; tiny people looking out through its brilliant walls. But this was what I saw everywhere I looked these days, little worlds where busy little people were busy getting on with things.

The news is followed by the weather.

The ice looked thick. I found a stick and whacked it; the stick broke. It was as hard as metal. The ice spoke. It said, You can walk on me. But along the bank, standing against a tree, was a wooden ladder; there are ladders against trees near all the German lakes, painted red and white. When someone falls through the ice you are supposed to lie out on the rungs and save them. Last winter when Bernadette was here she made me walk on the ice even though I wasn't skating. They all went round me in circles—not Sandy, he just fell and lay prone, feeling how he could lie on what even he knew was just water. But all I could do was walk stiffly. I just could not get over the idea that at some point the ice would melt and return to being a lake—so why wouldn't that be now?

188

Or maybe I should?

But then the phone would just ring and ring. Every day Bernadette asks me, long distance, 'When will you get here?' Sandy demands a turn and I get to listen to his breathing. Eventually he says my name, Dadda. Dadda come, he says. Dadda come? Then there's Fred, who just holds the phone. He's six now, I bloody missed his birthday. When I ask him how he is he says he's good. How was school? Good. Everything is good. Fred doesn't have any conversation on the phone, especially with someone who keeps asking how everything is. But, the thing is, he keeps holding it. He hogs it. I can hear him breathing too. Sometimes I don't say anything, to see what he'll do. But he just keeps holding on.

'Can I speak to Sally now?'

'Okay, Dadda,' he says. 'Bye, Dadda.' And off he goes. I can hear him, down the hall, calling her. She takes ages.

'Hi, Sal.'

'Hi.'

'Hi, darling.' Then I don't say anything else and so neither does she. An intercontinental silence—I can tell she's in danger of walking away and so I say, 'What've you been doing?' This is I know a gold standard conversation-stopper and, sure enough, she just lets it hang. I can hear her playing with the curly cord. I rack my brains. I'm empty, utterly vacant, and she just lets the silence grow, it's like being inside a circus tent, grey air everywhere.

Or, as a variation, she turns it on me; she says, 'What've *you* been doing?' Which I don't have anything to say about either.

Later, I talk again to Bernadette, who always says at this point, 'Hang on, I'll shut the door.' They're staying at her mother's house, where she can get some help. The extension is in the study. 'Well, she's hanging in her room, you have to

189

talk through the door. Says she's reading but I don't think so.'

'That doesn't matter.'

'No.'

'So what *is* she doing?'

'Reading—what can I say?'

'So what d'you *think* she's doing?'

'The counsellor told me to let her do anything safe. So that's safe. I asked if it's okay to let her brood and she said, yes, let her brood for a bit if she wants to. So I'm letting her.' I hear a sound on the line, a kind of science-fiction sound, a faint echoey clicking and I know that this is the satellite having a cigarette break, high there above the planet, shifting onto its other elbow or something—effortlessly bouncing my words and hers back and forth across ten thousand miles or whatever it is. 'She's stopped being rude. It's scary. She puts her washing in the basket—this is the new phase. She empties the machine. I never have to ask her to do anything.'

'And she's being nice?'

'No, I wouldn't say that.'

'No. Okay. And is she going to church?'

'What? No. What on earth made you think that?'

Because I've considered it myself. But I don't say so. I don't say anything, if I can help it. I'm like Fred, all I have to say on any given subject is, Good. I just want to hear the breathing.

'I'm afraid of her,' says Bernadette.

'Oh, come on, there's nothing to be afraid of.' This statement, heavy with genius, is faultlessly transmitted by the satellite—I can tell that there's a programme deep inside the thing that could send an Error message; that could hold my words and have a taped voice say to me, Do you really want this utterance to be transmitted? But then a minimum-interference let-the-market-decide super-programme judges that it will be best for the bullshit to walk and so Bernadette listens and hears.

Eventually the words fade.

Yes, eventually we figure a way to move the conversation forward and then finally we get to where we hang up. 'Night, darling. Night.' Kisses, coming wet-sounding down the line. But the hang-ups are only pauses, she'll be phoning me tomorrow, about the same time, and maybe tonight again even.

So should we be—afraid? Of this little woman, this old girl of thirteen years, who when confronted with a threat to the idea of herself has enough sense of the essential, of the right order of things, who grasps the knife and, with one all-or-nothing chance, plunges it correctly without fail into the bloody centre. Who is instantly showered in knowledge of the red kind, which gets on her skin, which hardens on her face. Who then figured the next steps. Who is alive without a scratch on her and wasn't raped—and yet who has a life on her hands. At thirteen, to be the cause of death. Personally, I didn't even *see* a dead person until I was in my late twenties and then it was a died-of-old-age. I've never killed anyone, not even in the drunk-driving days. I've never even actually hurt anyone.

Well, not physically.

I am definitely going to spend more time with her. I am going to devote myself to her. Not that she needs it, now. But I am going to anyway. Definitely.

I don't think I'm cold enough yet.

So I sit down here nights, or I walk around the block, in a teeshirt—along to Café Krone for bread in just a tee, where they all stare at me like I'm an escapee. Actually, it's not that bad, only minus one or something, minus two, and if you stop saying *Brrr it's freezing* and just walk around in it, well, as long as it's not for too long it's no big deal. But you mustn't think I'm doing penance or something. No, this isn't penance.

I just have to keep coming down here, I think, down to this lake, down to this jetty, and stand around here for a bit among the trees and just be near the ice. Be near the water. I don't mean to study the stillness—the zen of trees, fabulous. No, I just need to cool down a bit. To get a bit colder.